Alberta Church

Measure for measure

A Novel. Vol. 2

Alberta Church

Measure for measure
A Novel. Vol. 2

ISBN/EAN: 9783337101176

Printed in Europe, USA, Canada, Australia, Japan

Cover: Foto ©Andreas Hilbeck / pixelio.de

More available books at **www.hansebooks.com**

MEASURE FOR MEASURE.

CHAPTER I.

WHAT'S IN A NAME?

IT was like waking from a bad dream, when Beatrice found herself standing in the well-lighted hall of Wynthorpe House, hearing light words around her, marking down engagements on her card, and then joining the whirling throng in the dancing-room. Oh, if she could always take life on the surface! and never seek to pierce into its deeper recesses, through thirst for joy, or dread of sorrow!"

She tried, at any rate, to appear to take

life on the surface, and she succeeded. She was more recklessly gay than she had been since the conclusion of the affair with Captain Denbigh had given a check to the overstrained vivacity of her manner. On this night people said that Miss Clyde had resumed her flirting ways; but if it was indeed so, it was from no " catching at shadows," as formerly, but from the effort to conceal something—to fly from something—what, she feared to think—strove not to know.

Of course, the officers of the 121st were not absent from this entertainment; some changes had taken place in the regiment during the last six months, and the new arrivals, bearing no resentment against Beatrice for her treatment of their favourite, Captain Denbigh, she could find amongst them adorers enough, if she chose to give them a little encouragement.

She danced a good many times with a

Mr. Ashton, a rather empty-headed youth, but an excellent dancer, and amusing also from his transparency. True, his conversation sounded very poor, after that of Lionel Constable; but Lionel Constable seemed determined not to talk to Beatrice, and she endeavoured to persuade herself that she was quite satisfied to be neglected by him. Yet she never lost sight of him, and could have counted accurately the number of times he had danced with Dora Lyttelton. She could not, however, discover any devotion in his manner to Dora; indeed, he devoted himself to no one, and looked graver and more thoughtful than usual.

He did not ask Beatrice for more than one valse, and during its continuance not a dozen words were exchanged.

The Collingwoods were at this party, and Beatrice, after one of the dances, found herself seated in a group formed by Mrs.

Collingwood, Mrs. Constable, Amy, and Amy's friend, Agnes Gresford, who had been a bridesmaid. Lionel and Mr. Carleton were hovering about the circle, as well as Mr. Ashton, who was waiting impatiently for his next dance with Beatrice.

"Who got the sixpence in your cake this morning, Amy?" asked Mrs. Collingwood; "I know Miss Clyde had the ring."

"Dora Lyttelton," answered Amy.

"I should not think the omen will prove correct," said Mrs. Constable, "unless she is very difficult to please. At any rate, if she remains unmarried, there will be a good wife lost."

"I am sure," said Mrs. Collingwood, "I recommend matrimony to all young people, and no one has a better right to be heard, for I have tried it twice."

"Flattering to us," said Mr. Carleton.

"No, indeed," returned Mrs. Collingwood, who was fond of sham battles, "not at all; you are all bad enough; it is only our powers of adapting ourselves to circumstances, and bringing out the best parts of you. All husbands may be made into good ones by a little proper management."

"That says much for the docility of the men," said Mr. Carleton.

"Nothing of the sort," returned Mrs. Collingwood, "but for the ability of the women; and, by the way, Mr. Lionel Constable, I have a crow to pick with you. What did you mean by keeping Mr. Collingwood up last night smoking bad cigars with you?"

"They were not bad cigars, but first-rate Manilla cheroots, I assure you," said Lionel, "and Mr. Collingwood appreciated them, whatever he might tell you afterwards."

"Ah, Mr. Collingwood is not yet reduced to order, I fear," said Mr. Carleton, laughing.

"You know nothing about it," returned

Mrs. Collingwood; " he was unfortunately, for once, induced to follow a bad example, but it will not occur a second time. As for Mr. Constable, he needs a great deal of managing to bring him to anything like order, and I shall not recommend him to any of you young ladies."

"I think I shall look out for a lady of mature years," said Lionel; "she might be more likely to improve my character, and I should certainly stand in greater awe of her."

"Ah, you may sneer at age, you young men," said Mrs. Collingwod, laughing, "but we know better than to heed you. You see what you will come to, Miss Clyde, Miss Gresford, and Amy. Gentlemen may sneer as they will, however—happily, we know our rights."

"I declare, I meant no dispraise of maturity," said Lionel; "I think women charming at all ages, and each age has its peculiar attraction. Nay, the only woman I ever felt seriously inclined to fall in love with was seventy."

"I am not going to be talked over—I know what you meant," said Mrs. Collingwood; "I know you despise a woman after she is twenty."

"Twenty!" exclaimed Mr. Carleton.

"Yes—twenty. At least, you recognize no age between twenty and forty."

"Well, if we do not, that is because no woman ever owns to any age between," said Mr. Carleton.

"How dare you say so, you absurd man?—I will tell Mrs. Carleton of you. Talking of ages, however, I think the bride and bridegroom to-day were very well matched. She is twenty-four, I hear, and he thirty. Indeed, the whole match seems most suitable."

"According to Mr. Newton," said Mr. Carleton, "they are both perfect beings, and, of course, perfectly suited to go together."

"I should think that cannot be said of many couples," said Agnes Gresford; "I am sure if I were a clergyman I should be miserable at the thought of so often tying people together to be wretched."

"What a very morbid idea you must have formed of matrimony," said Mr. Carleton; "I never heard such a dismal theory from a young lady."

"Well, it is dismal to think of being fast bound for ever," returned Agnes. "I felt quite sorry to-day for Helen, to think she could never be free again."

"There is the Divorce Court, you know," said Mr. Carleton.

"Oh, how horrid!" exclaimed Agnes; "I am sure nothing could ever free one after the solemn words spoken in a church. I never was at a wedding before, and it seemed to me as if we were all being bound in some way or other, as well as Helen, from merely listening; and I am sure Miss Clyde felt just as solemn as I did —did you not?—was it your first wedding, too?"

Beatrice started, and gave an inaudible answer.

"Well," said Mr. Carleton, "if the marriage ceremony is so overpoweringly solemn in a church, Miss Gresford, when your own turn comes you should try a register office——"

"And that would not seem like a marriage at all," returned Agnes; "I should not feel bound in the least."

"Not bound!" exclaimed Mrs. Collingwood, with some eagerness; "I can assure you, you are as fast bound by a register marriage as in a church. You would find it hard work to undo the knot, I can tell you; and Mr. Carleton ought to know that."

"Very likely it is so in reality—I don't dispute it," said Mr. Carleton; "only I maintain that a young lady devoted to Gothic architecture and stained glass, as I see Miss Gresford is, would be less likely to fancy the ceremony binding, and we were only discussing a matter of feeling. Besides, one often hears of irregularities——"

"Irregularities!" exclaimed Mrs. Collingwood, speaking faster than usual, and with a heightened colour, "there are no more irregularities than there were to-day at church. I am sure I ought to know, and to be able to give an opinion on the subject; and I may say with truth that a registrar is just as conscientious as a clergyman, and as little likely to suffer anything wrong or underhand."

"Still, it does not seem the same thing," said Agnes Gresford; "does it Amy?—does it, Miss Clyde? I am sure you both understand what I mean."

Amy seemed afraid of answering, but Beatrice, who had been gradually turning very pale during this conversation, and who saw that Lionel's eyes were fixed upon her, replied in a hurried voice,

"Yes, but no feeling could make the reality less certain."

" The knot, once tied, is fast enough, depend upon it," said Mrs. Collingwood. "I am sure my poor Mr. Cartwright always felt it to be so; and I have often known him low-spirited after having married a pair that he thought unsuitable, or likely to be unhappy; for I don't deny that mysterious marriages take place oftener in register offices than in churches, and I could tell some curious stories that have come to my knowledge. Not that I ever tried to pry into professional matters—there is nothing, I can tell you, young ladies, that puts out a husband more than that. And Mr. Cartwright was most particular in every way—

indeed, over-scrupulous, it seemed to me, for he never, from ill-health, or be the weather what it would, neglected to go to his office when required, or allowed anyone to act for him."

During this long speech, Lionel Constable's attention had been irresistibly fixed upon Beatrice. In addition to her paleness he noticed a painful contraction of her forehead, and a visible trembling of her fingers, which played with her bouquet.

He fancied also that at the name of Cartwright she started, and that her agitation continued to increase whilst Mrs. Collingwood was speaking. She glanced nervously round, and then gave an appealing look to Mr. Ashton; but at the moment he did not see her, being occupied in watching the board upon which the names of the dances were written, and which was being changed.

" But what mysterious marriages did you

hear of, Mrs. Collingwood?" asked Agnes; "do tell us a story."

"My dear, there is not time; you must go and dance," said Mrs. Collingwood; "another time, perhaps, I may be able to tell you some curious circumstances."

Beatrice, who had succeeded in gaining Mr. Ashton's attention, now rose, and saying to him in a strangely artificial voice, "The heat is unbearable here; will you take me to the hall?" placed her hand upon his arm.

Her departure caused a little commotion in the group, as she was seated slightly behind Mrs. Collingwood, who was not a very easy person to pass.

"We are too many for Miss Clyde, I suppose," said Mrs. Collingwood, when Beatrice had gone; "she strikes me as one of those young ladies who are never so happy as in a *tête-à-tête*."

Lionel Constable felt himself wince under

the words, and, hearing the notes of the
next dance strike up, he escaped from the
circle by leading away Agnes Gresford as
his partner.

Puzzled as he was by the strange emotion of Beatrice, he did not, however, seek
her, in the hope of gaining any clue to the
cause of it; for he was too much provoked
by seeing her carry on what appeared very
much like a flirtation with Mr. Ashton,
and by hearing the comments of Mrs. Carleton and other people upon her conduct,
to own to himself that he felt any vivid
interest in her. At supper he was near
enough to her to hear her laugh, and her
voice, which was pitched unusually high, a
sign with her—he had become aware—of
hollow gaiety. He could see, too, a light in
her eyes which did not please him, though
it added brilliance to her beauty; how different from the sweet radiance in which he
had basked on the evening of his return,

when she had been so happy and gentle,
and her voice, attuned to its own low, subdued. key, had sounded so full of quiet
mirth !

After supper he did not dance much, but
lingered in the hall, watching the various
couples who, tempted by the soft moonlight,
were strolling on the lawn and amongst the
shrubberies outside. He saw Beatrice and
Mr. Ashton go out together, and presently
they returned and stood in the doorway,
near which he had placed himself. Beatrice,
he fancied, seemed desirous of attracting
his attention, but Lionel would not heed
her, and he answered slightly some observation she made to him.

The first bars of another dance just then
sounded, and Beatrice turned quickly to
Mr. Ashton with the words:

"This is your gallop with Miss Heywood,
Mr. Ashton; pray don't miss any of it, for
she is a very good dancer. Don't mind

me, I am not going to dance, and mean to
stay here for a little air. I dare say Mr.
Constable will take care of me."

Mr. Ashton raised some objections, but
Beatrice could do pretty much as she liked
with him, and he soon left her to look for
his partner.

Lionel, utterly bewildered by the evident
desire of Beatrice to remain with him, inclined more than ever to consider her a
thorough coquette, felt for the moment
unable to address her in the light tone suitable to the situation.

She too was silent, and when he looked
at her he saw that all her forced brilliancy
had vanished. She was looking depressed,
sad, and somewhat agitated, and, with a
thrill of pleasure, he became conscious that
with him she could cast aside the veil of
conventional gaiety, and dare to appear her
natural self.

Somehow, in a very short time after

Lionel made this discovery, he and Beatrice were walking in the shrubbery, speaking little, but both of them feeling a certain pleasure in being together. When they did speak, it was only to make some commonplace remark upon the occurrences of the day. Beatrice, however, seemed to grow more and more absent, and she answered one or two questions of Lionel's quite wide of the mark.

At length, after an interval of silence, she said, *apropos* of nothing,

"Mrs. Collingwood is quite as great a talker as you described her; is she in the habit of speaking about her late husband as she did to-night?"

"This is the first time she has mentioned him, in my hearing," said Lionel.

"Cartwright was the name, I think?" said Beatrice, with a little effort in her tone, and at the same time fastening the refractory clasp of her light burnouse; "do you know what he was?—she talked so much about professional affairs, as if she had known a great many secrets."

"He was a solicitor," said Lionel; "I know nothing about him, for I never heard of the lady till she became Mrs. Collingwood. They lived in London, I believe; and, from what she said to-night, I conclude he was a registrar; but if you are interested in his history, I have no doubt I can gather plenty of it from Mrs. Collingwood."

"Oh, no," said Beatrice, hurriedly; "it was amusing to see the way she fired up about register marriages."

"She was shocked at Miss Gresford's idea that they were not very binding," said Lionel.

"I dare say she thought her foolish," said Beatrice, "for being so overpowered by the ceremony in the morning."

"It is an impressive affair," said Lionel; "but I suppose, if one went to a great many weddings, one would become hardened. As for me, I am always afraid of looking at the bridesmaids, fancying they will not like being caught in tears."

"They don't always cry," said Beatrice; "I am sure I was too hard-hearted to shed a tear."

"No, but you looked paler than usual, and quite as much impressed as any one there. And as for crying, I fancy you are not a person whose tears lie very near the surface—it is girls like Agnes Gresford, who have never known a sorrow, who weep for sympathy."

The last few words were said with some emphasis, and Beatrice felt their implication, and experienced, as she had sometimes done before, a sense of Lionel's power to penetrate beneath the superficial crust of her manner, and to guess that a secret suffering was harrowing her very soul.

An intense longing came over her to tell

him that she was unhappy, to pour forth
the sum of her griefs, that she might enjoy
the relief of the sympathy she knew he
would give, and receive, perhaps, the counsel
that he, a clever man, might afford.

But she checked the desire quickly—to
indulge it might lead to unknown evils—
nay, it was madness in one like her to seek
to increase his interest in her. His eyes
were fixed upon her, and she could not
avoid his look of mingled inquiry and
tenderness. Yes, tenderness, which she
could not mistake; and as she recognised it,
and felt the warmth and truth of the feeling which the look betrayed, the yearning
to say something that might explain the inconsistencies in her conduct, which she knew
puzzled him, and checked the growth
of his kindly regard, increased to intensity,
and the effort to subdue it became an almost physical pain. Lionel meanwhile was
sorely tempted to declare the feeling which

she called regard or friendship, but which, he could no longer conceal from himself, was passionate love.

Standing alone with Beatrice in the moonlight, with her hand resting, half trembling, on his arm, her features softened and shadowed by an emotion she could not restrain, and he could not understand, he could not recall the prudential reasonings which had made him, not half an hour ago, decide that she was not the sort of woman he should wish to call his wife. Just now he only felt that she was beautiful and unhappy, and full of feeling—that to rouse that feeling for him, to lessen that unhappiness, to shelter her against every ill, to wrap her in his strong protecting arms from every breath of possible harm, would be perfect bliss. But he did not speak; steps were heard along the gravel, and Beatrice, at the same instant, proposed returning to the house.

He was not sorry; the moment she spoke, he awoke to the consciousness that he was in an excited state of mind, in which no decision could be safe. Besides, she had changed—her trembling emotion was passed, her light tone had returned, and a few words she addressed to some one they met were almost flippant. Piqued and provoked, angry with himself for wasting upon her so much earnestness, he conducted her in silence to the house, and gave her up in the door-way to a partner who was searching for her.

He returned to the dancing-room, engaged partners for the rest of the night, and endeavoured no longer to watch or think of Beatrice. But she was not a person to be forgotten, or to remain unobserved. Occasionally he caught the flash of her eyes in their hollow merriment, or the sound of her cold, clear, ringing laugh fell upon his ears; and at the close of the evening, when leaning on Mr. Ashton's arm, she passed him on her way to the carriage, her glance rested on him for a moment.   She started as she met his eyes, and with a bow and a "good night," she moved on; but that momentary, half-conscious, wildly mournful gaze haunted him through the night, and made him recall with minuteness and painful curiosity the peculiarities of her speech and demeanour during the past day.   What could her strange emotion mean, shown on so many occasions which appeared little likely to have roused in her anything stronger than indifference?

CHAPTER II.

EVEN AND CHEERFUL.

"I REALLY think, Amy, if you have no-thing particular to do this morning, you must take me to call upon the Clydes. I felt quite ashamed when I saw Miss Clyde last night," said Mrs. Collingwood, after the un-usually late breakfast at the Laurels the fol-lowing day.

Amy professed her willingness to go, and then Mr. Collingwood, turning from the window, where he had been talking with Lionel, said,

"If it would not be improper, I should

wish to go also. I have often heard of
Wynthorpe Palace, and I believe it contains
some great architectural curiosities. I am
a novice in such matters, but I think useful
information is frequently gained by a visit
to places of this kind. Yes, Miss Amy,
one is never too old to learn, and in my
time youth was not instructed and highly
educated as it is at present. And as I was
observing, if there is no reason why I should
not accompany the ladies, I feel very
strongly inclined to visit this interesting lo-
cality."

Mr. Collingwood was a man of about the
middle height, with an upright figure, slen-
derly formed, but endowed with a comfortable amount of flesh. His features were
rather handsome, after a regular, inexpres-
sive type, and he looked as if he ought to
have worn powder and a pig-tail. His
dress was very neat and precise, and he
spoke in a slow and emphatic manner, that

seemed to indicate something very important in the matter of his discourse. Young
people were apt to call him prosy, and older
ones resented his seizing upon so large a
share of the conversation.

"Oh, of course you can go, Mr. Collingwood," said Amy, "Miss Clyde left Mr.
Clyde's card for you."

"I should not wish to thrust my acquaintance upon any one," said Mr. Collingwood; "perhaps it would be more in
accordance with the rules of social life if I
were to send my card to Mr. Clyde."

"You need not think anything of that, I
am sure," said Amy, "if you wish to go,
for Mr. Clyde is not a person who goes out
much."

"Well, I have no desire to stand upon
my dignity," returned Mr. Collingwood;
"and my wish to see the Palace is very
powerful. I am fond of antiquities, Miss
Amy; it is singular how much we may

read in them of the wisdom of the past,
which we are too apt to forget in these
days."

"If you are fond of antiquities," said
Lionel, "there is a curious piece of Roman
pavement in the field-way to the Palace,
which I shall be happy to show you. I
cannot trust Amy to tell you its history
properly—she never remembers dates."

"Oh Lionel! when I am sure I know
every stick and stone in the parish, and the
history of every ruin within twenty miles!"

"You will go in great force, I think,"
quietly remarked Mrs. Constable; "of course
I shall remain at home."

"Mother, did you intend going to the
Clydes, if I had not gone?" said Lionel, in
a half whisper, a minute later.

"No, Lionel, I stayed up too late last
night to care for much exercise to-day,"
said Mrs. Constable; "besides, Dora Lyttelton promised to come over to let me know

how they all are at the House, after the
excitement of yesterday."

"That Miss Clyde is a remarkably fine
young woman, I must confess," said Mr.
Collingwood—"a very fine young woman:
she reminds me a little of Miss ——" mentioning one of the actresses of his youth;
"you remember her, I daresay, my dear
cousin," turning to Mrs. Constable, "in the
days when theatres *were* theatres. What
powers she had!—and she was a sweet pretty
creature, and sang very sweetly, too, any
little song that was introduced. I recollect
her well in 'Sweet Kitty Clover.' I can
recall the archness of her expression—you
would have thought she was Sweet Kitty
Clover herself—ah! that was worth listening to, Miss Amy.

> 'Sweet Kitty Clover—she bother'd me so,
> Sweet Kit-ty Clo-ver she both—er'd me so-o.'

"Miss Clyde sings beautifully," said Amy;
"and she acted splendidly in some charades

we had last autumn—indeed, I believe she can do anything she tries."

" I cannot see the resemblance you speak of, Cousin Sam," said Mrs. Constable; "and indeed I don't think a comparison between a young lady and an actress at all desirable for the former.   I am afraid, however, Miss Clyde's manners have sometimes approached too closely to one's ideas of people of that kind—I was sorry to see her flighty way of dancing last night, and flashing about her eyes."

" Still she always looks a perfect lady, mamma," said Amy, "her appearance is so distinguished."

Lionel turned upon his heel, and left the room by the glass door that opened into the garden.

He was angry with his mother for the cool depreciating way in which she spoke of Beatrice—irritated with Mr. Collingwood for presuming to admire her—whilst even

Amy's praises struck him as being too patronizing. Perhaps, if all the world had fallen down in silent adoration at the feet of Beatrice, he might have been satisfied— nothing less would content his craving to feel that she was placed on a pedestal before which he might worship without discredit to his judgment. Generally, he had enough confidence in himself; but now, almost for the first time in his life, he was conscious of a weakness that dimmed his clear-sighted-ness, and injured his reasoning. He longed to see her again, yet entertained little hope of gaining any clue to the contradictions of her character. If she said three words one day which seemed to promise him admit-tance behind the veil, she said a dozen the next that increased his perplexities.

He loved her, in a great measure because she was not common-place, and readily un-derstood like an ordinary woman; yet his heart would have rested more satisfied had

her speeches and her demeanour contained
less to pique his curiosity.

"I think my young friend Lionel appears
not insensible to Miss Clyde's attractions,"
said Mr. Collingwood, after Lionel's departure; "I observed some singular glances of
his last night, though perhaps he was not
so outwardly attentive as some of the
young lady's admirers."

"Of course, my son considers Miss Clyde
very handsome and attractive—he would
be blind otherwise," said Mrs. Constable,
rather stiffly; "but I feel sure he has no
idea—I think not—I hope so—a barrister
can seldom afford to marry early"—in a
more undecided tone—"and Miss Clyde is
not a wife for any but a rich man."

"Yet I noticed her dress was very simple
last night," said Mrs. Collingwood —
"nothing but that flimsy tartalane, not even
silk under it, and not a single ornament—

but it might, to be sure, be affectation of simplicity."

"She hardly ever wears jewellery," said Amy, "but I have seen beautiful things in her dressing-case."

" 'Beauty unadorn'd, adorn'd the most,'" spouted Mr. Collingwood; "but, I fear, that is a precept the young ladies of the present day are inclined to disregard. In our day, cousin, the young ladies displayed their slender figures, and we had sometimes a glimpse of a beautiful ankle. Now those enormous excrescences that are the mode entirely conceal some of the most graceful lines of the female figure; and as to ankles, the sweeping dresses would lead one to suppose that they were meant to hide elephant's feet——"

"This is Mr. Collingwood's satirical way," said his wife. "I tell him he looks from a wrong point of view—a pretty girl is a pretty girl, let her dress as she may,

and all the crinoline in the world would
not make Amy or Miss Clyde look a round-
about like me. And then, as to feet, I know
last time I was at Brighton I saw more
ankles displayed than I ever did in my
young days, and so did Mr. Collingwood,
though——"

" I think the less we say about them the
better," said Mrs. Constable, gravely, " in
these days of looped-up skirts and Balmoral
boots."

Soon after luncheon, the party set out on
their walk to the Palace; but at the entrance to the fields a division took place.
Mrs. Collingwood was afraid of cows, even
the most harmless ones, and declared she
would not go through any fields where they
were likely to be; if Amy did not mind,
they would go by the lane and the road.
Perhaps her terror about the cows was in
this case a little strengthened by the fear
lest a dress which she had put on, as the

newest London fashion, to dazzle the eyes of Mrs. Clyde, who was, Amy had told her, a connoisseur in costume, should be damaged by contact with any bushes or brakes, or torn in any climbing of perilous stiles.

Mr. Collingwood, of course, could not miss the Roman pavement, but he was loth to part with Amy, who proved a much more attentive and docile listener than Lionel; and Lionel, having himself a fancy for a little private conversation with Mrs. Collingwood, and forgetting that his sole excuse for coming at all had been that he might explain the Roman pavement to Mr. Collingwood, proposed that Amy should take his part of *cicerone*, and that he should instead escort the cattle-fearing lady through the lanes.

"You were mentioning last night some curious stories you had heard about marriages," said Lionel to Mrs. Colling-

wood, when they had walked some dis-
tance.

"Yes, but they happened a long time
ago, and my memory is not very good—I
daresay I confuse them together. I remember, however, one couple being married at
the register office, and it was found out
afterwards that the woman's first husband
was only just dead, and that it was to avoid
scandal amongst her friends that she married there instead of in a church. He was
much beneath her in rank, and her first
husband had left her all his money, and it
was supposed that she had coaxed him out
of it, to the prejudice of his own relations,
so that of course she could not have done
such a barefaced thing as marry another
man before he was cold in his grave—all
his relations would have cried shame
against her. You see, Mr. Lionel, though a
register marriage is just as regular as a
church one, it is easier to conceal. And as

for being binding, I am sure this poor woman would have been glad enough to be free again, for the man behaved shamefully to her, even beating her, and trying to get possession fraudulently of money that had been settled on her. It was through her attempts at getting her rights that Mr. Cartwright came to know her history, but he never told me the name. I am sure my blood used to run cold at hearing of her treatment, though it was no more than she deserved. You wonder, I suppose, Mr. Lionel, at my saying this—yes, I can read your countenance, you are thinking here is this woman who has married a second time, and she abuses another poor wretch who was led to do the same—'The faults of our neighbours'—No, you need not interrupt; but I would have you know the cases are different—I don't object to any woman marrying again after a decent interval—and I remained a widow myself several years after I lost poor Mr. Cartwright, and it was not for want of opportunities."

"Oh, I don't doubt that for a moment," said Lionel; "but may I ask how many years it is since the miserable marriage you have been referring to took place?"

"Why, it cannot be less than fifteen," said Mrs. Collingwood; "I have heard other cases of unhappy matches, but I cannot recall them just now; and I have often known Mr. Cartwright low-spirited, from the fear that he had married people who ought never to have gone together, which proves that he thought just as much of the responsibility as a clergyman could do. Indeed, he had a very high idea of the duties of a superintendent registrar, which he was, and I never could persuade him to depute his authority to anyone; and yet sometimes he was put to great inconvenience for a man of his habits—he was not of the active, restless turn of Mr. Collingwood, for our house was a long way from the office."

"You lived in London, I think?"

"Yes, our house was at the west, but Mr. Cartwright was registrar of St. Benedict's district in the city, and the office was in Fetter Street. I have been in it: a dingy, gloomy place, enough to make any bride lose heart when she found herself there. Oh, I assure you, Mr. Lionel, I like myself a wedding in a church, with a crowd of friends about, like the one yesterday—only I am vexed when an ignorant little chit declares that a register marriage is a bit less binding."

Whilst this conversation was going on between Mrs. Collingwood and Lionel Constable, another of rather serious import was being held at Wynthorpe Palace.

Beatrice and her father did not meet until luncheon-time, as Mr. Clyde had

ridden into Railton early, before Beatrice
had made her appearance. The meal was
a *tête-à-tête* one, as Mrs. Clyde was still in
her room; and whilst it lasted few words
were exchanged. But afterwards, when
Beatrice was about to leave the room, Mr.
Clyde called her back, and announced that
he had something to say to her.

Beatrice had been in rather more cheerful
spirits on this morning; the dreaded wedding was no longer in perspective, and her
observations had assured her that the man
she considered her friend had no intention
of throwing himself away upon Dora Lyttelton, however much his mother might
desire it. But her father's solemn speech
made her heart at once sink within her, and
she sat down again in undefined dread.
Mr. Clyde's next sentence was almost a
relief to her, though it roused her indignation.

Her father accused her of giving cause

for speculations of various kinds, amongst
her acquaintances, by her uncertain mode
of behaviour and contradictory moods.

"I hear," he said, "that yesterday your
depression in the morning was most marked
—you were pale, and agitated, and with
difficulty kept up anything like attention to
what was said to you; whilst in the evening you were so wildly gay that you
shocked sober-minded people."

"Papa," said Beatrice, colouring, "why
will you listen to silly gossip like this? I
am sure no one has any business to make
remarks about me, and still less to abuse me
to you."

"It was not likely that any one would
abuse you to me," said Mr. Clyde; "but I
happened to be in the library at Railton
this morning, and I suppose I was unseen,
for I heard much said about you that I
would rather not have heard."

"And why did you not show yourself,

papa, and stop the chattering of a set of giddy boys? It was not like you to listen in secret, and it was unjust to me."

"In the first instance, I could not have shown myself, and afterwards there would have been an awkwardness," said Mr. Clyde, with some hesitation; "besides, it is of importance to me to know what is said of you. You know how exceedingly desirous I am that no one should be able to call you a flirting girl."

"Which I suppose they did call me?" said Beatrice, quickly.

"One of the giddy boys, as you name them, plumed himself upon being high in your favour, and the rest teased him, and warned him that you were fickle. But that is hardly the worst in my opinion. I am still more annoyed that you give rise, by your melancholy, for the supposition that you are a prey to some hidden sorrow—the victim of some tyranny and oppression—

unrequited attachment, &c.   It is thought
by one that you try to excite sympathy by
your variable spirits, and another put down
your visible agitation at the wedding to a
disappointed affection for Mr. Heywood, and
your flightiness in the evening to desperation."

"Papa, this is too ridiculous — only
worthy of your laughter.   No one who
knows anything of me could ever have imagined that I sighed for Helen Lyttelton's
lover."

"That may be; yet it is no matter for
laughter.   It is highly objectionable that
conjectures of *any* kind should be made
about you; and by a little carefulness,
more uniformity of manner, you might
avoid it.   You ought not to be suspected of
any secret sorrow—the report might, in
future, lead to very unpleasant remarks;
the world might form an opinion, injuri-
ous——"

"Always appearances!" exclaimed Beatrice, impatiently; "they have been the
bane of my life—the cause of all our
troubles."

Mr. Clyde turned very pale.

"Beatrice, forgive my reproaches; you
have endured much, and perhaps my weakness—nay, I know, it ought to have been
conquered, but I am too old to alter, and
you must make the effort, without which all
is useless. My dear child, you have been
good—very good, lately, and you are exposed to many temptations. Do not renew
your folly of last year; and, on the other
hand, do not lay yourself open to a pitying
curiosity. Be even and cheerful, I entreat
you, my child, by all the considerations that
have influenced you before."

"But it is so hateful to cut and square
one's manner and one's words, feeling all
the time a deceitful wretch. It is easy
enough at times to be desperately gay,

the excitement carries one through ; but to be *even and cheerful* when one's heart seems breaking—oh ! papa, it is hard, indeed ! And yesterday, when I hated being where I was !—if only mamma had not insisted on my going."

" Beatrice, you have a wonderful power of self-control, and I have seen you exert it on occasions far more trying than yesterday, which was not, so far as I can see, attended by anything very formidable."

" Some one is coming, papa—there are steps on the terrace—let me go into the drawing-room."

" Of course—but you will remember what I have said ? "

" I will be as cheerful and as insipid as I can," said Beatrice. "I will appear an ordinary young lady, without any cares, except about my dress."

" Do not be mocking, Beatrice," said Mr. Clyde, in a hurt voice.

"Dear papa!" exclaimed Beatrice, "for-give me—I will—indeed—I only mean to please you;" and she went up and kissed him, and then left the room.

Mrs. Clyde was in the drawing-room, and in a most gracious mood—inclined to make herself agreeable to the visitors from the Laurels ; and in the presence of the stream and the torrent, as Lionel had called the Collingwoods, there could be no lack of conversation, or, at any rate, of noise. Beatrice acquitted herself very well, yet Lionel fancied at first that she was slightly constrained, and he observed a flush upon her cheek, much deeper than her natural delicate colour. It had, in fact, risen to her face during the short but painful dia-logue that had just occurred, and the excite-ment of meeting visitors had fixed it there. Mrs. Collingwood chatted away to Mrs. Clyde, in a way that lady considered very entertaining ; but she declared afterwards that she had been quite shocked at seeing a woman of the age Mrs. Collingwood was represented to be, such a dreadful bunch of a figure, and with the outlines of her features so completely lost in fat.

Mr. Collingwood expatiated upon his admiration for architectural antiquities; and some one proposed that he should be taken into an old dining-hall, now used as a laundry, in order to look at some curious mouldings and brackets.

Accordingly, leaving Mrs. Collingwood and Mrs. Clyde in the drawing-room, the rest of the party moved out upon the terrace, as the dining-hall was more readily reached from the outside than by going through the house. Amy attached herself to the two elder gentlemen, and Lionel and Beatrice followed together. Beatrice, however, kept pretty close to her father, and resisted every attempt made by Lionel either to linger behind, or to stand

talking in a corner of the hall. Lionel
hardly knew why he wanted private conversation with Beatrice; it was not likely
that she would say anything that would
lessen his perplexities about her. He was
determined, however, to introduce Mr. Cartwright's name, and to see whether it affected
her in the same manner as it had appeared
to do the night before.

"Mrs. Collingwood has been telling me
some of the tragical stories she referred to
last night," he said, when they were standing
together in the doorway, waiting for the
others, who were lingering a few paces off.
The sunshine streamed through the door-
way, falling full on the face of Beatrice,
whilst Lionel watched intently.

"Indeed!" she said, "stories of that kind
are often interesting; did you hear anything very terrible?"

"Something of Mr. Cartwright's mis-
givings at having joined together a couple

who were extremely unhappy afterwards—
the man beating the wife, &c."

"Oh, that is very common; I need only
walk into the village any day to hear a
story of that kind; I thought you were going to tell me something more romantic—
the abduction of an heiress at least."

There was just then a pause in the flow
of Mr. Collingwood's speech, and every word
Beatrice uttered could be heard by the rest.
Her tone was one of perfect indifference,
and Lionel could not trace any kind of
expression on her face. The emotion of
the past night must have been caused by
something quite different from the mention
of the name of Cartwright, and her after-
queries must have been made in the lack of
a subject for small talk.

"You inquired last night," continued
Lionel, in a lower voice, "what Mr. Cartwright was. He was, as I told you, a registrar, and I have heard all about him this

morning—he had a London district, St. Benedict's."

"Did I ask you?" said Beatrice—"you have a good memory for common questions. Yes, I remember being struck by Mrs. Collingwood's mention of her former husband; but don't you think this is an awkward subject for us to choose in the presence of Mr. Collingwood? In his next pause he will hear we are still discussing poor Mr. Cartwright, which may be unpleasant to him, so pray reserve whatever stories Mrs. Collingwood told you for another time; and if they only refer to the beating of wives, I don't care to hear them."

"Undoubtedly," said Mr. Collingwood, drawing nearer the door, "we have improved since those days—the appliances of science to common life—I beg your pardon, Miss Clyde, I trod upon your dress, I was carried away by the subject that has been

engaging our attention—not perhaps a very
interesting one to you; young ladies live in
the present and the future, they seldom
care for the past. It is when years ad-
vance, Miss Clyde, that we begin to think
of those that have gone before us. But
what a beautiful prospect you have from
this terrace!—indeed, I may say the charms
of nature and art combine to render this a
delightful abode."

When the party re-assembled in the
drawing-room, Beatrice chatted away in a
friendly, simple manner to every one; she
listened to Mr. Collingwood's solemn opinions, and submitted to be teased by Mrs.
Collingwood, in the style that lady thought
proper to adopt to all young ladies; altogether, she was as tranquilly happy in appearance as her father could desire.

But when the visitors had gone—Lionel
inclined to think he was a fool, for troubling
himself to discover remote causes for what

had probably been only a woman's capricious manner—she uttered a sigh of relief, and, going up to her father, said,

"Were you satisfied, papa?—was I not polite and agreeable—neither too merry nor too dull?"

"My dear Beatrice, your manner was perfection," said Mr. Clyde; "and believe me," he continued, with more tenderness, "I appreciate your difficulties. I watched you attentively to-day, and your conduct only proves how admirably you can control yourself; it is hard, my child, but in time it will be natural. If only I could hope that happiness would ever repay you," and passing his hand caressingly over her head, he left her.

Beatrice went to her own room, and looked out across the fields and lanes that lay between the Palace and the Laurels.

"It is hard and dreary," she said to her-

self; "and when my confidence is sought,
I must deny it. I must never make a
friend."

She dashed away some tears from her
eyes, and remained long gazing from the
window, full of a vague longing, an unquiet
pain.

Fresh from her father's reproofs and
entreaties, she had, on this day, made
a powerful effort to act as he would ap-
prove; but she was far from being able to
persevere in the course he had laid down
for her. At times she felt almost bitter
against him; it appeared to her that she
was treated with injustice, and that no one
had any right to prescribe to her any set
form of manner. If the wildness of desperation had power to give her relief, if in
exciting amusement she could alone lose
the sense of her unhappiness, surely the
indulgence ought not to be denied her! It
was overstrained authority and harshness,

on the part of her father, to chide her because she could not always maintain her spirits at an even and cheerful level.

CHAPTER III.

AN UNANSWERED QUESTION.

THE marriage of Helen Lyttelton was followed by a succession of rural gaieties, got up chiefly for the amusement of the visitors who were staying at Wynthorpe House. Beatrice threw herself into all the pic-nics, riding parties, impromptu dances, that went on, with something of the zest she had shown the preceding winter; and if she did not flirt so decidedly with Mr. Ashton as she had done with Captain Denbigh, she yet allowed both him and Fred Lyttelton to talk nonsense to her in a way which sober-minded people condemned as most reprehensible. She had not indeed forgotten her father's remonstrance, and at times she endeavoured to make her conduct agree with his wishes; then again she was urged on by a feeling of desperation to do what in her own heart she despised herself for. She dare not pause to think; in excitement she found refuge from thoughts and feelings which must at all hazards be crushed.

Lionel Constable continued against his will to watch her, and against his reason to love her. And although Beatrice appeared systematically to avoid him, there were still moments when all but the thinnest disguise was cast off between them, and each felt, in the presence of the other, an indefinable sensation, blent of rapture and suffering.

Thus a fortnight passed, constantly meeting, perfectly determining not to seek each other, yet ever drawn together by some

subtle, mutual influence. How Beatrice
spent her hours of solitude during this
period, it would require volumes to tell;
let it be enough to say that she strove to
make such hours as rare as possible, and to
drown in a whirl of society the misery that
oppressed her, and goaded her on to actions
which she loathed. Verily, the ordeal
through which she was passing was full of
bitterness, and of torment so intense that
many a gentle, tender woman might have
sunk under it and died; but Beatrice had
a nature at once strong and buoyant, and
even now her anguish was sometimes relieved by an exquisite thrill of passionate
joy, almost enough to compensate her for
all the after-woe it cost her. There were
storms in the domestic circle to be encountered, in addition to her own exclusive
mental sufferings; disputes between her
father and mother about her conduct; the
veiled wrath of the one, the still more pain-

ful indulgence and ill-judged sympathy of
the other.

And hanging over all was a dread, more
than a dread, the certain prospect of an
inevitable fate, which might be near, might
be distant, but which was surely striding
on, to deprive her for ever of even the
flashes of happiness which pierced occasionally through the surrounding gloom.

The Collingwoods, meantime, were still
at the Laurels, the day of their departure
being repeatedly postponed. They were
people who enjoyed social gatherings, and
country pleasures were new to them; and
in spite of a few eccentricities, they were
agreeable enough additions to a party,
whilst Mrs. Collingwood was a sufficiently
easy chaperon to be generally acceptable.
The day before the one finally fixed for
them to leave the Laurels, there was a
pic-nic to Glendale Abbey, the party con-
sisting of the Wynthorpe House family and

guests, Amy and Lionel and their visitors, Beatrice Clyde, the Carletons, the officers, and a few other young people from Railton.

Some, amongst whom was Beatrice, rode; Mr. Ashton, of course, devoted himself to her, and, until the Abbey was reached, entirely monopolized her. Luncheon was the first business of the day, and every one was soon occupied with the arrangements. Beatrice, however, was an exception; she sat a little apart, and looked pale and wearied; she often did look very pale now, and, when not animated, had a worn expression, which caused her detractors frequently to remark that Miss Clyde was beginning to look old and *passée*.

"Mr. Lionel, Mr. Lionel!" called out Mrs. Collingwood, "do bring me that vinegar directly. I cannot think what makes you gentlemen so stupid. I wish I had kept Mr. Collingwood here, but I thought you young people ought to make yourselves useful. I declare that mustard is not half mixed. Here, Mr. Collingwood, you must come and help me, these young men are good for nothing—I think they must be all in love. Ah, I see he is talking to Miss Clyde, so never mind; it will do her no harm to have a little rational talk, instead of listening for ever to those boys."

Mrs. Collingwood discoursed on, sending her vassals hither and thither, and making more noise than anyone in the circle; whilst her husband was pouring into Beatrice's unheeding ear a series of reminiscences of former excursions in which he had taken part.

"A very pretty ruin, I can see, this is, Miss Clyde, but not so highly finished as Scarscombe—were you ever there?—no? —well, I assure you, that is most delicate; the carvings are, I may say without exaggeration, and in full confidence, for I was told so by Brett, the architect, exquisite.

Yet, I will not deny that youthful impressions go a great way, Miss Clyde, and are
not to be dismissed as valueless—yes, I saw
Scarscombe when I was young, and I
remember—dear me, it seems like yesterday—how merry we were! A young lady,
something like you, Miss Clyde, only with
lighter hair, and perhaps a little fuller in
the face, sang us one of Tommy Moore's
songs—we all sang Tommy Moore's songs
then—and afterwards one of the young
fellows gave us, ' Oh, believe me, if all those
endearing young charms'—I daresay, a
young lady like you, acquainted with all
styles of music, may have heard it. Those
sweet old ballads are far superior to the
new ones in my estimation, Miss Clyde;
but there again we must take into account
our youthful impressions. Ah, youth is a
fine thing—we can none of us deny that."

The proser was at this moment interrupted by Lionel Constable, who, seeing

the weary look on Beatrice's face, approached to her relief, and drew her away, on the pretext of exploring a neighbouring portion of the ruin whilst luncheon was being prepared.

But Mr. Ashton, never far distant from Beatrice, on seeing her rise, attached himself to her, and Lionel, having no fancy for taking part in a trio, soon left the two together; so that Beatrice was compelled again to listen to Mr. Ashton, an infliction for which she was not in the mood, though by her previous encouragement she had lost the right to complain of it.

He began telling her of some former love-affairs of his—always a favourite subject with him—and thus the time passed till they were summoned to luncheon.

When the regular tour of the abbey commenced he was still by her side; helping her to climb difficult places, gathering ivy for her on mouldering walls, at the peril of breaking his limbs, and entertaining her with his stories.

The abbey was really beautiful in itself, and made more so by its situation. Standing on a smooth platform of turf—smooth, at least, except where buried walls gave inequalities to the surface—near the banks of a gurgling stream, crossed by a bridge of dark grey stone, nearly as old as the ruin, and surrounded by forest trees, beneath which winding walks led up the rising ground, sheltering the building on two sides, or down into romantic shady dells—the whole place was one well suited to while away a summer's day in. And the just changing tints of the trees added brilliancy and variety to the scene, whilst the soft September breeze, sighing gently through the woods, gave a tinge of sentiment—a sort of foretaste of sadness to the impression produced.

"Miss Clyde," said Mr. Ashton, after a

pause, during which Beatrice had been taking in the beauty around her in a lazy, dreamy manner—" do you think I could stand on that pinnacle?" pointing as he spoke to the summit of a broken pillar.

" I don't know how you could get there."

" Oh, there are steps within that door-way—don't you see them?—and then a passage above, between those windows—do you see?—and then, of course, one must mount on hands and knees. Shall I do it?"

" I should not like to see it," said Dora Lyttelton, who was in a group at a little distance, and caught the last sentence. " It would be most dangerous, and frightful to look at."

" I don't know," said Jessie; " I think it would be awfully jolly—do go, some of you —Mr. Curzon, suppose you try."

" No one shall go before me," said Mr.

Ashton, who was rather vain of his activity; " only say the word, Miss Clyde."

" Well, you would look rather well standing there," she said, laughing—" so go."

Mr. Ashton needed no further inducement—off he went, and in a few moments appeared standing on the top of the pillar. The position was really perilous; and Beatrice, as she looked, felt that, had anyone she cared about stood there, she should have suffered agonies of nervousness. But Mr. Ashton stood his ground firmly, and, after the hurrahs of the beholders, descended in safety.

Jessie Lyttelton and a few more girls were now eager in inciting other youths to the enterprise, but they were not very successful."

" Come, Mr. Constable," said Jessie, at last—" I am sure you will not be behind in a thing of this kind. Do go, and we will subscribe to give you a reward."

"Tell me first what it is to be," said Lionel, pressing forward into the circle, from the place where he had been standing with Mr. Carleton.

As he did so he caught Beatrice's eyes fixed upon him, and saw her lips form a word which he interpreted as "Don't," though no sound issued from them.

Carrying on an exchange of banter with Jessie, he drew nearer Beatrice. She did not speak to him, however, but, assuming a decided air, said to Jessie—

"Don't recommend any more foolish things—it was quite enough to see Mr. Ashton. Such displays are only fit for schoolboys, and we ought to be ashamed of encouraging them."

But Jessie would not be satisfied.

"Well, I must say you are all cowards if you refuse to go. I did not know you were so easily frightened, Mr. Constable; your life must be very precious to

yourself or some one else. If I were you,
I should not be afraid, remembering the
old proverb———"

"I should be ashamed to think so lightly
of myself," said Lionel, laughing. "I am
very precious to myself, whatever I may be
to other people, and you are quite at liberty
to think me cowardly—I daresay I am."

Everyone laughed, for cowardice was one
of the last things of which Lionel Constable
could have been accused.

The mild voice of Dora Lyttelton rose,
however, in his defence—

"There is more moral courage sometimes
in refusing a post of danger, than there
would be physical courage in accepting it."

"An undeniable truth," said Mr. Carle·
ton; whilst Lionel bowed low, acknowledg-
ing the compliment.

Beatrice's lip curled with scorn as Dora
spoke, and she turned away from the group.
Mr. Ashton did not accompany her, for he

was just then engaged in defending himself against Mrs. Collingwood's charge of fool-hardiness; and Lionel, seeing this, actuated by an irrepressible impulse, followed her.

They neither of them knew how it was that they remained together the whole of the afternoon, nor how they became lost in the woods, nor could they ever exactly recall what they talked about.

Beatrice was gentler than usual in man-ner and conversation, and the desire she had shown to prevent Lionel from placing himself in danger had made him feel that she had some peculiar interest in him, and that at any rate the friendship, which had lately seemed checked between them, still existed on her part. More than this, he became aware, for the first time, that he had a certain power over her. The hours passed rapidly, almost deliciously, in spite of many a misgiving. If only life could be spent thus—in rambling amongst these

woods—sitting beneath their thick shade,
watching the flickering golden light through
the transparent leaves, Beatrice, at least,
would have been satisfied. So she fancied,
possibly with truth.

But Lionel could not be thus content—
he knew now that he must speak ; the im-
perious moment would not be delayed; he
could not part from Beatrice without knowing on what footing they were in future to
stand to each other. At this instant he
believed she loved him—he could not look
in the speaking depths of her dark, passionate eyes, and doubt it.

They were walking now, somewhat late
in the afternoon, along a narrow path
above the stream ; the branches of the
over-arching trees occasionally half obstruct-
ing their passage. They had been silent
for a long time, senselessly happy at being
together, yet each conscious of a vague
emotion of unrest beneath the surface cur-

rent of pleasure. Lionel spoke at last:—

"Do you remember the afternoon when I found you reading Humboldt, and when I recommended 'The Lotus-eaters' as a more fitting study?"

"Yes, certainly."

"Do you still hold the doctrine, 'There is no joy but calm'?"

"I don't know—it was not so much a doctrine as a wish. Perhaps you think I have since then acted as if I liked anything rather than calm. I know people have been fancying me full of excitement, the gayest of the gay."

"I have never fancied so," said Lionel; "I think I can read you better."

His tone was low and grave, and Beatrice felt his eyes full upon her. She could not deceive *him*—could not, with him, keep up the semblance of a light heart.

"You are right, perhaps, in your reading; but if I am unhappy, surely I am not

wrong in wishing to present a calm front
to the world."

" But it is not a calm front," he answered,
gravely; "you only perplex the world by
alternations of extreme gaiety and visible
depression—you perplex, at any rate, those
who feel the most real interest in you.
You act in a way that makes some who
would be your friends condemn you—
pardon me," he checked himself suddenly;
" I have no right to speak to you in this
way."

Beatrice did not appear offended: her
cheek flushed, and she walked on with cast-
down eyes; but when she did raise them,
all the fire was quenched out of them, and
there was an appealing, deprecating glance
in them, that stirred the deepest chords in
Lionel's heart.   All his soul was in his
voice, as he said,

" Miss Clyde, you cannot conceal from
me that you suffer.   What your grief is I

dare not ask, unless you give me the right; but if I could in any way lighten the burden you bear, I would give the last drop of my heart's blood to do it—and count myself happy and honoured."

Was it a shadowy feeling which Beatrice experienced now? Was the sudden flash of delirious joy which burst upon her a deceitful meteor, which was to vanish, and leave her to the utter blackness of her destiny? Oh! could it not stay—this delicious moment, when all the imagined bliss of a life-time seemed gathered into one exquisite drop? Ah! it must endure; it must be real —misery could never return to her—Lionel loved her!

Yet for one moment only the transport lasted—the one moment in which alone she had felt the full sense of all the happiness of which life was capable—gained a glimpse perhaps of joy attainable only in some more favoured state of being.

There was scarcely any pause before she replied,

"No one can help me—once before you offered help, and I refused—it is the same now."

"No, not the same," said Lionel; "then I did not know the secret of my interest in you—then I offered help blindly—now I offer it because the sight of your unhappiness poisons my whole life—"

"You—whose enjoyment of life was always so intense," said Beatrice, half bitterly.

"*Was,* but is not—I was proud in my happiness once, Beatrice, I own it to you—before I met you, believing myself sufficient for myself, I went serenely on my way. Fool that I was!—full of notions of universal affection—good-will—I know not what—notions which you afterwards pushed to the utmost, whilst at the same moment you were teaching me their unreality."

"Stop," said Beatrice faintly, " I cannot

hear you talking in this way. You must return to your old ideas—to my ideas—they are the only safe ones."

"They are a dead letter," said Lionel, passionately. " Beatrice, when I am standing by your side I can think nothing, believe nothing, but that I love you."

Beatrice could not answer. Again there was the rush of joy through her veins—again the sickening reaction followed—she felt powerless—trembling in every nerve.

" Beatrice," continued Lionel, yet more impetuously, " you know I love you—you must have known it long—give me hope that you will some time love me in return."

" Oh, spare me, spare me!" murmured Beatrice, covering her face with her hands. He tried to touch them, and to withdraw them from her face, but she shrank from him in real fear.

" You do not know—you do not know!" she repeated, trembling.

" No, I do not know, but you will let me know—you do not hate me, Beatrice—I cannot think you do — you will let me penetrate this mysterious grief which oppresses you. My love—my darling—it cannot—*cannot* be so very terrible that it will not yield to my love."

His tone sank into a low, tender whisper, so unlike anything that would have been expected from his clear, ringing, cheery voice, that the change filled Beatrice yet more with the sense of his deep, heartfelt devotion ; yet she shrank still further from him—dreaded the faintest touch of the hand whose clasp would, at that same instant, have thrilled through· her nature with unspeakable bliss.

She tried to speak —to frame words which should convince him that he must stifle for ever that love, which would have blessed her, but which she must renounce — the obstinate syllables would not come, and before she had succeeded in her attempt the branches were brushed aside, and Mrs. Collingwood and Mr. Carleton stood before them.

Now that other eyes were upon her, Beatrice had no difficulty in collecting herself—she was again the self-possessed Miss Clyde, capable of answering Mrs. Collingwood's questions, and laughing at Mr. Carleton's remarks.

It was time to start homewards, and Mrs. Collingwood and her companion were engaged in searching for the missing members of the party. Beatrice and Lionel joined them and proceeded in quest of Jessie and Mr. Curzon, who were discovered at last, sauntering towards the general rendezvous.

In the bustle of departure, Lionel had no opportunity of exchanging words with Beatrice, and during the ride home Mr. Ashton was by her side. She listened to his talk, and gave answers as in a dream, carrying on, all the while, her separate train of thought; living over again the last few minutes of her interview with Lionel, hearing his words, feeling his presence, yearning to speak—to assure him that she understood, that she loved him; yet, at the same time, dreading to be again alone with him—fearing to hear his voice, but catching wildly at its lightest echo.

Sometimes he was near her—she felt he was, though she did not see—would not look at him; once his hand caressed her horse as it had done that evening when he had been annoyed by her philosophy.

Filled with deepest agony and wildest rapture was that ride home through the twilight—agony that seemed at moments scarcely endurable—rapture that at brief intervals refused to be crushed back and quenched by cold reason.

To still excitement by counter-excite-

ment, Beatrice urged her horse to his mad-
dest speed, till her companions could scarcely
keep pace with her; once Lionel was close
by her, so close that she could not help feeling that his eyes were fastened upon her—
but she would not look, though she would
gladly have prolonged that moment for
ever.

At length she stayed her speed; she was
approaching home, and must part from the
rest of the party. Mechanically she went
through the leave-takings, and then prepared
to turn into the lane leading to the Palace.

Jessie and Fred, who had called for her
in the morning, were to accompany her to
the door, so further escort was unnecessary.
Lionel, bound to attend to Amy and his
visitors, was compelled to say good night:
he held out his hand—grasped hers with
fervour and passion—and they parted.

The moment Beatrice entered her own
home she became aware that there had

been an arrival in the house. There were strange packages in the hall, and servants were busy carrying them away. A sudden foreboding seized her, and hurrying forward she stooped to read the name on a hat-box —she saw the words, " Mr. Menteith."

How she reached her room afterwards she never knew, but when she had reached it—had thrown herself upon the ottoman in the window, silent witness of so many scenes of tumult and of pain—she buried her face in her hands, and there issued from her lips, wrung, as it were, from the very depths of her being, a long, repressed, agonized wail.

CHAPTER IV.

MR. MENTEITH.

"BEATRICE, Beatrice, what are you doing here in the dark? I expected to find you dressed, and ready to come down-stairs."

There was no answer, and Mrs. Clyde advanced further into the room and saw, at length, the crouching form on the ottoman. Utterly crushed it looked; lifeless and motionless—but at a louder exclamation from Mrs. Clyde, the bent head was raised, and a face disclosed to view, the sight of which would have been enough to harrow any mother's heart—so terribly wan and worn it was—so marked by conflict and woe!

How long Beatrice had lain postrate in her agony she did not know; the time seemed to her, in remembrance, like years, though it must have been short in reality.

She rose now, as if waking from a troubled sleep, and said, in a low anxious voice,

"It is not true? Oh, mother, say it is not true!"

"My poor darling! you know, then: yes, Mr. Menteith is here. He arrived just before dinner; the letter which he sent before him has been lost, it seems."

"But, so suddenly! Why so suddenly?"

"I don't know—business has brought him, I suppose. He did not intend coming, when the former mail left, so he could not let us know till he arrived in England. But, child, you must dress, and make yourself look less miserable. You cannot meet your father with a face like that—I will send Larkins to you."

" No, no, mamma, I can dress myself;" and Beatrice began hastily to unfasten her riding-habit, but her fingers trembled, and all her strength seemed forsaking her. Mrs. Clyde took up an eau-de-Cologne bottle, and began nervously sprinkling her with its contents, and then brought her water to drink; but her attempts at usefulness were awkward, she was so much more accustomed to be cared for than to care for others.

Beatrice, however, summoned to her aid the innate vigour which she possessed, and, after a few efforts, was able to proceed with her toilet—again earnestly entreating her mother not to send for Larkins.

Mrs. Clyde was obedient to her daughter's stronger will; lighted the candles on the dressing-table herself, and began to search in the wardrobe for a dress. Beatrice did

not care what she wore, and submitted,
without remark, to her mother's choice,
though the dress selected was a more
recherché one than she usually wore in the
evening. Her hair, which had fallen loose,
was then hastily gathered into a net, fastened with gold pins, and, with her mother's
help, she was now ready to proceed to the
drawing-room. Her exertions had given
a flush to her cheek, and her wild eyes
glittered with feverish brilliancy. Altogether, though, to those who knew her, her
face bore marks of suffering, to unaccus-
tomed eyes the main impression it would
give would be that of beauty—beauty indeed of a rather fierce and startling order,
but perhaps, on that very account, all the
more attractive to some tastes. Her tread
was firm, and her lips compressed, as she
followed her mother into the room; yet
the lights dazzled her, and a film seemed
to float over her eyes, as she was led for-

ward by her father, and introduced to the stranger who stood near the fire-place.

He bowed, and muttered something, and then Beatrice sat down on the sofa by her mother, and listened dreamily to the conversation he was carrying on with her father. He was a man of perhaps five-and-thirty, but he looked like one of those people whose ages are extremely difficult to guess; for his face, though marked by strong lines, was one that never, even in boyhood, could have possessed the smoothness and roundness of youth. He was plain, and would have been insignificant, but for a considerable breadth of brow, just over the eyes, where the perceptive organs were well developed. The head was high, and rather narrow, and covered somewhat scantily with hair of a decidedly sandy hue, which, though evidently carefully attended to, had a tendency to separate into lank, obstinate-looking locks. The eyebrows and whiskers were of the same colour, and the complexion had the pale, pasty appearance which usually accompanies hair of this description. The eyes, of a light grey, were capable of varied expression; the nose was short and sharp, exposing to view a considerable portion of the nostrils; the mouth large, with full lips, exhibiting, when he spoke or laughed, a row of white and even teeth, the only beauty of the whole face. Mr. Menteith's figure was short and slight; the upper part smart, and rather well made, but the lower part was awkward; his legs being too small, and not symmetrically formed. He was dressed in a careful and gentlemanlike manner, and his bearing was that of a man who has seen a good deal of the world, though there was a dash of formality about it, which contrasted visibly with the ease that distinguished his host.

He talked well, and rather forcibly, but

his voice was not pleasant. It was pitched too high, and there was a sharpness in the way in which the words were jerked out, that seemed to betray either a bad temper or a nervous readiness to take offence.

The discussion between him and Mr. Clyde was of a business nature, but occasionally Mr. Menteith's attention wandered from the subject, and he cast upon Beatrice a glance of mingled curiosity and admiration; and when the conversation was over he approached the sofa, and drew a chair near the two ladies.

They were both in a silent mood, but by degrees Mrs. Clyde's reserve, or whatever emotion caused her silence, thawed, and she yielded to the sway of the stranger's agreeable talk, which had already, at dinner, rather impressed her. For he was singularly agreeable, describing well and pleasantly the scenery and mode of life in South America, with which he was well acquainted, having, for the last eight years, managed Mr. Clyde's business at Rio Janeiro.

Beatrice now heard, expressed in well-chosen words, an account of the gorgeous tropical scenery which she had so often, in fancy, enjoyed beneath the influence of her favourite Humboldt's magic pen. But the *vivâ voce* description, good as it was, did not charm her like the written one, and in a short time thoroughly wearied her.

Mr. Menteith readily perceived that her attention was forced, and now changed the subject of his talk. Instead of detailing his own experiences, he endeavoured to lead the conversation into a channel which would draw some remarks from Beatrice herself.

"You have been enjoying an excursion to-day, I hear," he said; "have you been very far?"

"Only to Glendale Abbey," answered Beatrice, "about ten miles off."

"You can see it from the Terrace on a clear day," added Mrs. Clyde.

" A ruin, I conclude; is it very beautiful?"

The question was addressed to Beatrice, but her mother answered it.

"It is considered so. Beatrice is too tired, I am afraid, to tell us much about it to-night. Did you enjoy your day, love?"

" Yes," said Beatrice, "it was a very pleasant pic-nic."

Her tone betrayed absence of mind, and Mr. Menteith looked fixedly at her for a minute. He moved his chair slightly, so as to bring himself nearer to her than to Mrs. Clyde, and said,

" Are you fond of such things? Do you like gaiety?"

" I like anything exciting," she answered, hurriedly—" a monotonous life is dreadful to me."

"I believe I should find it difficult to

bear myself," said Mr. Menteith, "but ladies are so different from us. And *you*, from all I have heard of you, can never, I should think, be at a loss for resources. One of your accomplishments I remember, though I only knew it by hearsay. I have not forgotten your music; and although you are so altered since the early days when I saw you last, that I should scarcely have known you, I trust you are not altered in that respect—you are still fond of music?"

"It is a great pleasure to me," said Beatrice.

"I fear to-night I must not ask to hear you—you are too tired perhaps?"

"No, not too tired for music," said Beatrice; and she rose, and went to the piano. It was a relief to her to have something to do, and she felt as if, in drawing forth the exquisite tones of the instrument she loved, she were appealing to and receiving the sympathy of an old friend.

She could not sing—she could not trust her
voice; but she sat down, and played for a
long time, giving vent to irrepressible feeling in tones which, though unintelligible
to her hearers, impressed them with a sense
of power and passion.

Mr. Menteith remained sitting by Mrs.
Clyde; he was watching Beatrice rather
than listening, admiring the skilful, intricate play of her white fingers on the
keys, rather than attending to the har-
monies they called forth. He was a man to
be affected more through the eye than the
ear; and there was not a single point in
Beatrice's charms, not an iota about her
personal adornment, that he did not take
in, and note with satisfied approval. He went
up to the piano, when she paused, and asked
her to go on—she complied, and he stood
behind her. He felt that there was meaning in the music, though without compre-
hending it, and even had it not been agree-

able to him, he would have chosen to pro-
long the time of listening.   It gave him
an excuse for not talking to Mr. and Mrs.
Clyde, and opportunity to study Beatrice,
and determine what line of conduct to
adopt towards her—for he had resolved to
please her; and though aware that his external advantages were not great, he
believed that women were less particular on
such points than men; and he knew that he
possessed certain powers of fascination,
which might make him acceptable to an
intellectual woman.

He saw already that music was, with
Beatrice, almost a passion ; and for that
very reason he determined to be frank
with her on the subject.   He knew she
would find out his want of enthusiasm and
knowledge, and he thought that an acknow-
ledgment of ignorance, and a blind admiration of both her ardour and her skill,
would be more likely to win her favour

than any attempt at half-sympathy So, when the piece he had asked for was over, he said,

" It must be very delightful to have such enjoyment in anything as you seem to have in music. I can enjoy listening to you, but I am quite aware that my enjoyment is nothing to yours."

" No one can judge of another person's power of enjoyment," said Beatrice; and she was rising, as if to prevent further remarks, but Mr. Menteith stopped her, saying,

" Oh ! not yet, unless you are tired."

And caring little what she did, she sat down again.

" I should like to explain what I meant," he continued. "I wish to tell you that, though I am sure I cannot appreciate music as you do, I can understand your delight in it thoroughly. If we wish to comprehend any person's pleasure in anything, we have only to compare it with our own in something we do understand, in order to enter into it entirely. Thus I can compare your pleasure in music with my own satisfaction in accounts."

Beatrice, in spite of her pre-occupation, was a little surprised by this speech, and she showed her surprise. He had startled her, and he had intended to do so.

"You are astonished," he said; "and it does seem a very earthly and prosaic comparison, but what can you expect from a business man?—and I do not see why we cannot exercise a love of harmony in one way as well as another."

"Nor I," said Beatrice; "and there is analogy, I suppose, between music and mathematics. Still—" she paused—she had no desire to explain her feelings to Mr. Menteith.

He waited a moment for her to continue —leaning against the piano, and looking into her face, but she did not go on.

"You think, perhaps," he said, "that the best part of music is feeling, and that I can find nothing in accounts to compensate for that. But there are other things besides music which can awaken feeling. If I chose I could tell you of several which have the power to rouse in me as many deep and varied thoughts and emotions as those which you can summon at will by the touch of your skilful fingers. I can understand, you see, though I cannot sympathise."

Beatrice did not answer; she thought the discussion of music and feelings had gone far enough.

He watched her in silence, and he observed her determination to drop the conversation. A gleam of displeasure shot from his light grey eye; then he said, in a quick tone,

"You are tired, I think, and I weary you with talking;" and he walked away to Mrs. Clyde.

Beatrice let her fingers wander idly over the keys for a short time longer, and then left the piano, and seating herself at a table, occupied herself with some work of her mother's. Mr. Clyde left the room, and Mr. Menteith was devoting himself to Mrs. Clyde, describing his voyage and his fellow-passengers—entering into the history of her complaints, and discussing new novels, with a discrimination not to have been expected from a resident in South America.

Presently Mr. Clyde returned to the room, remarking that it was late; and Beatrice seized the opportunity to remind her mother of the fact. Mrs. Clyde rose immediately, and said "good night" to her visitor with much cordiality.

Beatrice followed, going mechanically through the form of leave-taking; and then, hurriedly parting from her mother, she sought the solitude of her own room.

Miserable thoughts, and yet more miserable dreams, were her companions through the night—and, unrefreshed, she awoke in the morning to the tortures of a new day.

Lionel Constable, meantime, was not free from tormenting doubts and fears. Though he fancied he had seen in the looks and manner of Beatrice some marks of love for him, yet her anxiety to avoid explanations, her excited, unnatural demeanour, seemed to contradict the idea. Suspense was intolerable to him, and he resolved, at any rate, to see and speak with her before another day had closed.

If he were once alone with her, even for a few minutes, he knew she could not refuse to answer him.

In the afternoon of the day after the picnic he walked over to the Palace. He was ushered into the drawing-room, where he found Mrs. Clyde alone. It was so very seldom that Lionel had encountered her during his visits, that he felt slightly taken aback, and half-inclined to think that Beatrice had determined to avoid a private interview with him. He was conscious that all the embarrassment of a man in love was creeping over him, and that he was making himself just as ridiculous in that situation as the people he had been in the habit of laughing at. But Mrs. Clyde apparently saw no fault in him; she went on talking in a friendly strain, as if she were pleased to see him. He lingered out his stay, hoping every moment to see Beatrice enter the room—but she never came. In vain he told himself that if she did come he should have no chance of private conversation with her—just now, to see her, would be enough—he could not bear to leave without a single glance into her deep eyes, a touch of her little hand—in desperation, he said, at last, to Mrs. Clyde:

"I hope Miss Clyde is not tired, after our excursion yesterday; Amy and I have been planning a ride for to-morrow, and we hoped she would join us."

"I don't like these very long rides," said Mrs. Clyde. "Beatrice seems half dead after them—she was, last night; but where do you propose going?"

"Only to Scarth Hill, to see the view, and the old tower. Amy says Miss Clyde has never been there, and it is worth seeing."

"Well, I cannot answer for her engagements," said Mrs. Clyde; "and we have a visitor here now—however, I know it is a great pleasure to Beatrice to ride with you; and Mr. Menteith could go also, I suppose —so—you had better ask Beatrice about it yourself; she is walking in the garden— you can get on the terrace by that door."

Lionel needed no further invitation; he slipped through the door so rapidly, that Mrs Clyde, beginning another sentence to him, was surprised to find he had vanished.

" Well," she said to herself, " he was in a hurry, certainly—I dare say I ought not to have let him go—but it cannot do much harm. Only, if he really is in love with Beatrice, it will be a great pity. First Captain Denbigh, and then this fine, handsome young man ; just a fit husband for her—but it is no use thinking what might have been."

And Mrs. Clyde threw herself back luxuriously amongst her cushions, and returned to the perusal of " Heart Struggles."

Lionel Constable turned from the terrace into the garden, which enclosed one side and the back of the house ; but at first he found no trace of Beatrice.

He was just turning up a path which led to the hot-houses, when he caught sight of her coming out of one of them, accompanied by a stranger, whom he immediately concluded to be Mr. Menteith, the visitor mentioned by Mrs. Clyde. Who was he? And

what was his business here?—were two questions which instantly forced themselves upon
Lionel. Of course, he could not be a lover
without directly conjuring up a rival in this
guest whom Beatrice seemed to be honour-
ing by conducting on a tour of inspection
through the grounds. Of course he, the
stranger, could not be in the same house
with her without falling in love. Folly!
Lionel smiled in self-scorn, and dashed
angrily aside a rose-branch which stretched
across his path, as he found himself giving
way to these puerile fancies.

A glance, too, at the visitor satisfied him
that in externals he was far inferior to himself, Lionel Constable; and though too sensible to attach undue importance to personal
advantages, he felt, as probably any handsome man would have done, a sense of
pleasure in the consciousness of superiority.
Another look, however, at Mr. Mentcith
told him that, if in him he had to dread a

rival, he would find one by no means con-
temptible—there was a certain power about
the head, the expression, the whole bearing
of Beatrice's companion, which declared him
to be a man capable of compassing his
formed designs, and of driving straight
across the obstacles which might inpede his
course.

In another moment Lionel reached the
couple, who still stood by the green-house
door—had shaken hands with Beatrice—a
hasty shake, since her hand was quickly
withdrawn—and had been introduced by
her, in a hurried, embarrassed manner, very
unlike her usual self-possessed style, to Mr.
Menteith.

The few disjointed, unconnected sentences
which were now exchanged, did not deserve
the name of conversation.   Mr. Menteith
was too much occupied in scanning curiously
Lionel's face and form, to do more than
utter an occasional remark, and Beatrice

appeared scared and confused. Lionel was the most collected of the trio, and he soon mentioned the proposed ride to Scarth. Beatrice showed no eagerness on the subject, but did not decidedly refuse to go. Never had he seen her so uncertain, or heard her use such vague expressions.

" Well, I suppose I must tell Amy that you do not feel inclined for the ride," he said at last.

It was remarkable how ofter poor Amy's name was dragged into the matter, and how little she had to do with it in reality.

" No—not that," said Beatrice; "I should like the ride very much — I have never been to Scarth—but perhaps—Mr. Menteith —are you fond of riding ? "

" I like it well enough to be always happy to accompany you when you will allow me," said he. There was something in his tone, as he said the words, which made Lionel feel as if he should like to knock him down. What business had he to speak so, before Beatrice had positively asked him to go with her?

"Scarth is worth seeing, I believe," continued Beatrice; "at least the view is said to be fine—perhaps you will like to ride there?"

Mr. Menteith would be delighted, if he should not be considered an intruder; and of course Lionel was obliged to make some civil speech, assuring him that such would not be the case.

"I dare say papa will like to go too," said Beatrice; "he need not mount the hill unless he likes. It is steep, I believe, but we shall none of us mind that."

"You like hills," said Mr. Menteith to Beatrice, in a low voice; "I should be glad to show you mountains."

"Your mountains would be too grand for me, perhaps," said Beatrice, with a half-shudder; and turning to Lionel, she added,

"You may tell Mrs. Constable that the petunia she gave me now far surpasses hers —the flowers are splendid ! "

"Is it here ? " said Lionel, opening the green-house door ; " let me look at it, that I may give a correct report."

He passed close to Beatrice as he went in, and looked earnestly at her ; but her eyes were cast down, and a slight flush that rose to her cheek was the only sign that she had perceived his glance.

" Where is the petunia ? I cannot discover it amongst so many," he said, hoping to draw her attention to himself for a moment.   Beatrice entered the green-house, and Mr. Menteith followed her.   She pointed out the plant, expatiating upon its beauties with forced interest, and removing, with trembling fingers, one or two leaves that had fallen on the mould.

Lionel bent his head over the plant, so low that his face was close to hers.

"Am I to have no word to-day?" he said, seeing that Mr. Menteith's back was turned for a moment—"not one word with you?"

Beatrice shook her head, and then gave him a single glance—it expressed at once dread and entreaty, and a nervous shudder seemed to run through her frame.

He would have said she was a prey to mortal terror, but for another and different look that came into her eyes, as they met his—a look which he thought he could not misinterpret, and which thrilled through him, waking all his tenderest, most protecting impulses.

Filled with passionate love, most earnest pity, he longed to stretch out his arms, and take her to his heart, as her safest, surest refuge, from whatever mysterious evil harassed her — but they were not alone.

During the one instant that their looks

had met, Beatrice's face had crimsoned over—and ashamed, confused, and trembling, her eyes fell, and she drooped her head over the flowers. Recovering herself by a violent effort, she turned round, and made some remark to Mr. Menteith about the plant he was examining.

Lionel, convinced that there was no chance of a private interview with her that day, did not delay his departure; but, after making arrangements about the time of starting to Scarth the next morning, took leave.

As he turned the corner which led to the terrace, he glanced back, and saw that Beatrice was in the act of giving Mr. Menteith a flower she had gathered in the greenhouse. What did all this mean?

She might certainly give a flower to one of her father's guests without blame— Lionel, in former days, would have been the first to say, "Is it anybody's business?"

had any comment on such an action reached his ears. But now! and if that guest admired her, as he visibly did— if he received such a gift as a token of favour— then the case was altered, and the act was one of coquetry. Again, all that Lionel had seen, all that he had heard of Beatrice occurred to him, and he bit his lips, and strode angrily away. Was this the woman he could love and honour as his wife?

CHAPTER V

ANTAGONISTIC SPIRITS.

SCARTH HILL was an isolated eminence, standing nearly in the midst of the vale of Rothbury; the country around, as well as the lower portion of the hill, was well wooded, and only the extreme summit rose bold and bare, crowned with the solitary tower of crumbling grey stone supposed to have formed part of a hunting-seat of the Percies in days of old.

The weather was hot for September; the white mists of early morning had cleared away, and the sun, unobscured by a single cloud, shone full on the ancient building, as the riding party approached the foot of the hill. Beatrice had induced her father to join them. From some reason, known only to herself, she preferred having him with her, and during the whole ride she had kept as close to him as possible.

Lionel and Mr. Menteith exchanged a few remarks, and the latter attempted to make himself agreeable to Amy, but all the time the two young men were chiefly occupied in watching each other—each trying, perhaps, to discover a clue to the character of the other.

Mr. Menteith did not appear much at home on horseback; though not absolutely a bad rider, he found it necessary to pay so much attention to the animal he rode— a rather spirited horse of Mr. Clyde's—as to interfere a little with the part he intended to play during the expedition. Besides, when Beatrice, impelled by that fierce ex-

citement which often seized her on horseback, occasionally urged her steed to a mad
gallop, he found himself unable to keep
pace with her, and at the same time have
full control over his horse.

Mr. Clyde apparently saw his guest's dis-
comfort, for he expostulated with Beatrice,
though in a half-joking fashion, declaring
that she would weary herself, and everyone
else, before reaching the end of the ride.
Beatrice yielded immediately, and passed
the latter part of the way riding slowly,
almost silently, by her father's side.

The horses were put up at a cottage at
the foot of the hill, and Beatrice and Amy,
with Lionel and Mr. Menteith, prepared
to climb to the top. Mr. Clyde said he
should go round to another part of the hill,
where the ascent was easier, and wait at a
bench the woman of the house had pointed
out to him, until the others had explored
the tower, and seen all the views.

Mr. Menteith was more expert as a climber of hills than as a horseman—he found out the most direct ways of ascending, displayed considerable agility, and insisted on helping Beatrice over all the difficult places. Lionel, knowing that in general she scorned assistance, was surprised to see that she now received it without remonstrance, even when it was scarcely necessary. He stalked gloomily along with Amy, who was more silent than usual. At the top of the hill, however, her animation returned to her, and she pointed out with eagerness the different spots that could be distinguished.

"It is a beautiful view," said Beatrice; "but I don't think I care so much for that as for the feeling of freedom one has after mounting a height. One seems to breathe and live!" and she took off her riding-hat, and let the cool breeze blow against her cheeks.

Mr. Menteith stood by her, looking round on the scene for a moment or two; then he turned to her, and fixing his eyes on her face, lighted up by the flush of animal life imparted by fresh air, movement, and sunshine, he said,

" You have a strong love for nature, I see. If you can admire this narrow, cramped landscape, what would you say to our immense plains and waving forests ? "

Beatrice did not answer, but Lionel, who was standing near, and had heard the last speech, said to her,

"From all I know of your tastes, I should think you would prefer a view of this kind to one of greater extent and less variety. Besides, there are associations connected with this, and I know you value them."

" There are associations, too, with the scenery I have just been referring to," said Mr. Menteith; " there are memorials in

America of a bygone civilization fully as interesting as any of these relics of an age of barbarism," and he touched, as he spoke, the wall of the tower.

"Barbarism!" exclaimed Beatrice, "I cannot call any age barbarous which could boast a chivalry such as we know only by hearsay."

"I am sorry to differ from you," said Mr. Menteith; "but I cannot bring myself to think very highly of what was called chivalry in those dreary times of fighting and oppression."

"Chivalry is not quite extinct even now, I hope," said Lionel; "and probably we are all far happier than we should have been in the old chivalrous days; but still I agree with Miss Clyde in refusing to call the middle ages barbarous. It is true there was not much recognition of the real rights of human beings; and from all the ancient chronicles which have reached us we

gather that physical strength and beauty
were the only idols ; other merits were
barely acknowledged, or, at any rate, could
not make their way as they do in our
times."

Mr. Menteith pressed his lips together
with unusual firmness—then he said,

" Talent must have made its way more
or less in all times, but there were more
victims to their own genius then than
there are now. What epithet but that of
barbarous can we apply to ages when
witchcraft was believed in, and innocent
persons suffered for it—and when any discovery in science could be hushed up and
crushed by the decree of a bigoted church ? "

" Not crushed," said Lionel—"a true discovery was never crushed yet; truth always
will make itself felt, sooner or later."

" Yours is a hopeful creed, I know," said
Beatrice ; " however, I suppose we ought to
be glad we live in times when truth is pro-

fessedly worshipped.   Whether the worship
be sincere, we may judge for ourselves.
For my part, I am inclined to have greater
faith in the old homage to strength and
beauty—and   we   find   remnants   of   this
homage lingering in all primitive places.
Have you never remarked, Amy, how the
poor people here admire personal advantages—strength and activity?   It is quite a
mania with them—they think very lightly of
any book-learning or head-acquirements in
comparison."

"And I suppose you sympathize with
them," said Mr. Menteith, "as they express
the sentiments of the age you regret."

His tone betrayed something like pique
or annoyance, and Beatrice's countenance
changed as she heard it.

"If I do sympathize, I take myself to
task for childishness," she said ; "I should do
discredit to my teaching if I did not recognize the worth of greater gifts than beauty

and strength—gifts which at any rate bring more success," she added, with an accent of repressed bitterness.

"Come, Amy," she said, after an interval of silence—awkward, though no one knew why, " tell us the history of this tower of the Percies. You know all the legendary lore of the country, I am sure."

Amy began, and told what she knew, in a simple, rather picturesque manner; and if no one attended much to the narrative, it yet saved them the trouble of talking.

The tower had only been a hunting-seat, but there was a tradition that the builder of it had once converted it into a bower for his ladye-love, a novice whom he had stolen from the not very distant convent of Rothings. There was a tragical history of how the father of the damsel had discovered her knight, had chased him to the foot of the tower, and had fought him there, before the very eyes of the recreant novice—how the lover had fallen, and the lady had thrown herself from her window, in despair.

" Every old legend one hears is connected with some fearful crime," said Mr. Menteith, when Amy had finished.

" Were crimes more common in former times, I wonder ? " she asked—" or were they more known ? "

" They were more known," said Beatrice; " at least those committed by a certain class were. In these days it is different; the crimes of the poor are almost always brought to light, whilst those of the rich may remain hidden."

" Do you object to that as a fruit of over-civilization ? " said Mr. Menteith, looking at her curiously.

Beatrice coloured a little as she replied,

" One ought to object to anything which prevents justice. But in speaking of crimes, I believe I was thinking rather of those which are not punishable by law, but which reason tells us must be accounted for some day. Crimes which destroy happiness and life, by working upon the fears or the peculiar dispositions of others, must in reality be little short of murder."

"Reason surely scarcely told you that such would be accounted for," said Mr. Menteith.

"If I said reason, it was because I did not wish to use a stronger word," said Beatrice.

"I should like to know more definitely the nature of the crimes you allude to," said Mr. Menteith, in a subdued voice, gazing on Beatrice's flushed cheek and sparkling eyes with a look in which admiration and some less agreeable emotion were mingled.

"It is not necessary to enter into further particulars," she answered, "and this is but dreary talk. Let us try something else.

Amy, you are the youngest and lightest-hearted, say something merry."

Amy laughed, and declared, as people always do on such occasions, that it was impossible to be merry on demand; but gradually a different tone was given to the remarks. When the tower had been thoroughly explored, they all proceeded in search of Mr. Clyde; he was sitting on the bench, where he had directed them to look for him, and after a little more rest it was announced that it was time to start home-wards.

Lionel instinctively came forward, when the horses were brought out, to help Beatrice to mount; but at the same instant Mr. Menteith advanced. Beatrice turned away hastily from Lionel, and he fancied he saw a look of fear on her face—a look so sad and unfamiliar that it made his heart ache with a pity which was scarcely tinged with his own disappointment. She did not, however, accept Mr. Menteith's services, but having her horse brought near some steps, and standing on them, she sprang up by herself—Mr. Menteith hovering about her, arranging her habit, and lingering over the little offices he performed much longer than was at all essential. Lionel watched, in spite of himself; saw the restrained impatience which made Beatrice's features quiver, and, at the same time, marked the submissive way in which she passively endured Mr. Menteith's attendance.

During the ride home Lionel could not obtain a word from her ; Mr. Menteith never left her side. He had conquered whatever slight annoyance had crossed him on the hill ; now he was agreeable—nay more, interesting in conversation. Yet he never addressed himself to Lionel; and Lionel, having no mind to appear a sentimental hanger-on, attached himself to Mr. Clyde and Amy, and endeavoured to behave as if

neither Beatrice nor Mr. Menteith existed.
At the Lodge gates the riders separated:
Lionel and his sister pursued their way
home, and the others entered the Palace
grounds.   In the avenue they met Mr.
Carleton, also on horseback.

"I have been wanting to see you," he
said to Beatrice, after he had been induced
to turn with them towards the house; " I
was obliged to leave a message with Mrs.
Clyde.   We want you to support a sort of
entertainment at the Literary Institute to-
morrow evening—it is no use asking Mr.
Clyde, I know, but you are quite depended
upon.   You will come, will you not, and
stay supper with us afterwards?—the Lytteltons are coming."

"What is the affair to be?" asked Beatrice.

"A sort of lecture, to be given by a
very clever, amusing man who is staying
with Headly, the master of the grammar-

school. Where Headly picked him up I don't know, for he is not at all a likely person to be a chum of a book-worm like him. However, there he is, ready and willing to lecture for the public good, exhibit panoramic views of his own making, sing, dance, and I know not what besides, in illustration of his descriptions. Altogether the thing will be worth listening to, and you must not miss it—my wife quite expects you."

Beatrice looked uncertain.

" I should like it very much, but—"

" Perhaps your visitor might like to come too," said Mr. Carleton, looking back at Mr. Menteith, who was with Mr. Clyde. The latter immediately introduced the two gentlemen to each other — the invitation was given to Mr. Menteith, and in a minute or two it was settled that he and Beatrice should accompany the Carletons to the lecture, and return with them to supper.

"You may be able to judge of the truth of our lecturer's representations," said Mr. Carleton, after he had been made aware that Mr. Menteith had just come from South America, " for his entertainment is to be called ' Life in Southern Climes,' or ' Wanderings in Southern Seas,' or something equivalent."

" Then it will be rather stupid, I should think," said Mr. Menteith, whilst a look of annoyance, so slight as to be scarcely perceptible, passed across his hard features, " stupid, at least, unless exaggerated."

" Oh, we don't mind exaggeration in our behind-the-world place," said Mr. Carleton ; " the inquiring minds of our Literary Institute supporters require something startling to fill them—and I am not sure that the false ideas they get do them much harm, their imaginations generally require stimulating. However, if you hear anything very far from truth we elders are willing to be enlightened, provided the young ones get their fill of wonders."

" Then a good invention is the only thing needed to please a Railton audience?" said Mr. Menteith. " If I were to lecture upon Japan, where I have never been, I suppose I should be attended to."

" Certainly ; if you told sufficient crams. However, I see both you and Mr. Clyde are shocked at my loose principles, so I will reserve them for Miss Clyde. We have some sympathies, I know. She approves of fictions."

" Realities are so dismal," said Beatrice, "that it seems an advantage to lose the sense of them in fictions, whenever it is possible."

"And the power of doing so does not last very long with most of us," said Mr. Carleton.

" If it did," said Mr. Menteith, " there would not be much work done. In the world realities may be uninteresting, but they are necessary."

" Ah, you talk like a man of business ; a thing I have been trying to do all my life, and failed in," said Mr. Carleton. " I should have been a richer man than I am, if I had adopted your creed."

"But not a happier one," said Beatrice, in an undertone.

" I don't know about that," answered Mr. Carleton; " but here we are at the very door, and I must turn back. Good morning—to-morrow at seven we shall expect you," and Mr. Carleton rode off, refusing all invitations to enter the house a second time.

" Is Mr. Carleton a great friend of yours ? " asked Mr. Menteith that evening, as he and Beatrice were sitting together near the piano.

" He is one of the pleasantest people in the neighbourhood," she replied; " and I

believe—yes— I am sure I may consider
him a friend—he would show me any act
of friendship I might require."

"Probably he improves upon acquaintance," said Mr. Menteith.

"Most people do, who are worth anything," returned Beatrice; "but still I have
generally found that men like Mr. Carleton
please at once, though their higher qualities
are only discovered afterwards."

"He is a rather random speaker," said
Mr. Menteith; "I know that such men do
please ladies frequently, but I should have
imagined, from my idea of your character,
that you would have required something
different. However, I am glad that I
have gained some notion of what you do
like."

He looked full in her face as he spoke,
and there was something in his glance almost insolent. Beatrice did not blush, or
drop her eyes—she drew herself up proudly,

and said quickly, as if the words were forced from her:

"What my tastes are cannot really be of any importance to you—it will never· make any difference to you."

"Will it not?"—Mr. Menteith's voice fell to a whisper, and his look changed to one which was almost imploring, and which softened the harsh lines of his face—"you little know of what importance your lightest word is to me—I am not what you think me—what perhaps you have reason to think me."

The true feeling in his tone unnerved Beatrice; her haughty manner left her, and she began playing a loud fantasia to drown further conversation. Mr. Menteith sat just behind her, watching her intently— surveying her with greedy eyes. There was pain mingled with the admiring ex- pression on his face—pain and longing, and something that seemed like regret. But by the time she had finished, he had mastered whatever emotions were struggling within him, and his countenance bore its usual aspect. He asked her to sing, and she sang, for some time, without eliciting any remarks from him. At last he said, just as she had concluded a pathetic love-song,

"I wish we were not going to that absurd entertainment to-morrow night. These quiet evenings are so delicious, so much more delicious than anything I have ever known," and he glanced at the distant figures of Mr. and Mrs. Clyde, who were both absorbed in their books near the fire-place, and then drew his chair closer to Beatrice.

"Why absurd?" asked she; "I expect to be amused myself; but there is no occasion for you to go, if you despise the entertainment."

"You know that I fully intend to go,"

said Mr. Menteith—"I only mean that I think it a waste of time—I cannot stay here for ever, and every moment is precious to me."

"I like going anywhere," said Beatrice, "I am not at all a domestic person. People ought to be very happy, to be satisfied with a quiet life, I think."

"And are you so very unhappy?" asked Mr. Menteith.

"If I am, I do not mean to discuss my unhappiness," she said; "no satisfaction either to you or me could ensue from my doing so."

"You should not say that—unhappiness frequently only requires probing into, in order to disappear—yours will vanish some day, I venture to predict." Mr. Menteith looked confidently at her for an instant; but the shudder which visibly ran through her, as he spoke, somewhat disconcerted him, and he added, in a sort of deprecating manner,

"At least, I am sure you are not naturally formed for unhappiness; and all who have anything to do with you could never have the heart to cause you suffering —a man who did not strain every nerve to make you happy would be deserving of execration."

"All the efforts and all the will in the world cannot make another person happy," said Beatrice.

"I see nothing to prevent it," said Mr. Menteith, "certainly nothing in your case. Perseverance and devotion will be rewarded in the end — they must call forth—" he checked himself. "I can only see one cause to hinder them"—and he looked expressively and inquiringly in her face — "a reason which does not—cannot—*ought* not to exist."

Beatrice did not look at him—she occupied herself in putting aside her music; then, rising, she began to shut the piano, saying it was late. Mr. Menteith rose to help her, and, in closing the piano, his fingers touched hers—an impulse seized him, and he took her hand, and held it for a moment. At first she seemed angry and startled, but she did not remove her hand —it lay cold and motionless in his clasp. Suddenly he let it go, and muttering, " I will not take what is not freely given —at least not yet," he left her, and went up to Mr. and Mrs. Clyde to wish them " good night."

CHAPTER VI.

ERIN-GO-BRAGH.

IT was seven o'clock on the evening of the
following day, and a small party was assembled in Mrs. Carleton's drawing-room.
Mr. Headly and his guest, the lecturer,
had dined with the Carletons, as well as
Lionel Constable, whose sister was to come
afterwards with Beatrice Clyde and Mr.
Menteith. The Lytteltons, too, were
expected every moment, but the time spent
in waiting for them did not seem long, so
amusing was the stranger, whose stories
were never exhausted, whilst his humorous

manner appeared always changing—so that
even Mrs. Carleton, who was usually unable
to see a joke, was utterly taken out of herself,
and compelled to yield to the sway of his
merriment.   The entrance of the Lytteltons,
with   their   visitors,   Miss   Heywood   and
Agnes Gresford, only increased the noise
and laughter; and in the midst of a confused
hubbub of voices the party from the
Palace arrived.

Lionel's attention was now completely
fastened upon Beatrice; she was looking
pale and weary, almost subdued, and was
evidently unable to laugh and talk in her
usual manner.   Mr. Menteith was fully
occupied with her, but did not appear at
his ease; he looked reserved and distant,
and as if he rather despised the mirth of the
rest of the party.

Arrangements were now being made for
starting to the Town Hall, where the lecture
was to be given; and the lecturer was

urged by his friend to depart immediately, to be in readiness to begin, but he seemed in no hurry.

"Preparation, my good friend! 1 require no preparation : Brian Hope Desmond is not the man to turn cowardly, or lose his tongue when bright eyes are upon him. No, no—trust him for that—the beauties shall not be disappointed—he'll talk to them, and tell them the wonders of southern skies and the charms of southern shores till midnight. Keep the audience waiting! No, no, man —no fear of that!"

And Mr. Desmond moved leisurely, though not quietly, through the room.

"What is that man's name?" asked Mr. Menteith, as he gained a clearer view of him.

"I heard Mr. Carleton call him Desmond," said Beatrice.

"Ah, an Irishman, I conclude." Mr. Menteith gazed curiously at the receding figure of the lecturer, and was silent for a minute or so. He was unmindful even of Beatrice; for Lionel Constable had drawn near, and was speaking to her, before he was aware of his approach.

"Mrs. Carleton wishes you to go in the carriage with her, Miss Clyde," Lionel was saying; "may I take you to it?"

"Thank you," said Beatrice, glancing, half-timidly, at her abstracted companion. He started instantly, drew her arm through his, without either permission or resistance, and led her away, leaving Lionel looking rather blank.

Beatrice's eyes fell upon him, as she was turning from him, and again he read in them that sadness which stirred all the compassionate tenderness of his nature.

When would she speak to him? When should he succeed in withdrawing her from the mysterious power this stranger appeared to exercise over her?

Lionel went into the street—he and Mr. Carleton were to walk to the Town Hall; and in a short time they overtook the lecturer and Mr. Headly, who had not proceeded far.

Mr. Desmond was talking as vigorously as if he had been silent all day, and as if he were going to remain silent for the next two hours, instead of being expected to amuse an audience.

" Ha, Mr. Constable, is that you ? " he said, as Lionel drew near ; " you were looking after the ladies when I left the room. A splendid creature I saw you speaking to —a trifle pale and thin perhaps, but the real thing, and no mistake. By my faith, sir, I tell ye, I have not seen such a head set on such shoulders since I left Andalusia; and she's got feet and ankles to match, I'll warrant. There was a little whipper-snapper hanging about her, only fit for the like of her to tread upon. I did not get a

fair look at him, but his face seemed familiar
to me, and Brian Hope Desmond never for-
gets a face, be it that of friend or foe. Do
ye happen to know his name, eh?"

"I conclude you mean Mr. Menteith,"
said Lionel—"at least if the lady you allude
to is Miss Clyde?"

"Eh, now, don't pretend not to know
whom I meant; ye're a sly rogue, I see.
Menteith—well, I don't know the name any-
how. Is he a stranger here?"

"He is a visitor of Mr. Clyde's," said
Lionel, "and connected, I understand, with
his business in South America: he has only
lately come here."

"South America!—been living there for
some years?"

"I believe so—but really I know very
little of Mr. Menteith."

"And wish to know less—I see that.
Well, she's too good for him, that is easy
enough to see. She's fit to make a duchess

of, that's what she is, and worthy of an
Irishman. And there's blood in her air,
and that's what he's not got, be his name
Menteith, Macheath, or any fine Scotch-
sounding—eh, I beg your pardon, but ye've
no Scotch blood in your veins, I hope?"

"No," said Lionel; "have you a very
strong prejudice against the Scotch?"

"Not prejudice—no man is freer from
prejudice than the one who stands before
ye—what I say, I say from knowledge and
experience. I've seen Scotchmen in my
time, sir, and a close-fisted set they are—
self-righteous, too—blaming all little follies
in their neighbours, and setting themselves
up with a 'Stand by!—I am holier than
thou!' And that they call religion, the Puri-
tanic knaves! Brian Hope Desmond may
not be a religious man, but his religion
teaches him something better than that—
charity to all—that's the true law for men,
not for sneaking hypocrites. I may tell

you, as I would a friend, Mr. Constable, that but for a pitiful wretch of a Scotchman, I should have been in a far different position from that in which you see me. He—I don't mind giving you his name in full—Andrew Stewart Macgregor, did me out of some property that came to me through my mother. I grieve that her pure soul should have claimed kindred with such a beggarly crew—but it's a long tale, and I'll tell it ye another time—for here we are, and now for the Southern main! Give way, my boys—make room for the lecturer," and Mr. Desmond scampered up the steps into the Town Hall.

Lionel and Mr. Carleton looked round for the ladies, and found they were already seated. Mrs. Carleton had kept a place for her husband, but Lionel had to hunt one out for himself. He succeeded in getting into the second row of seats, where some officers of the 121st were sitting.

An invitation to supper at the Carletons' afterwards had induced them to grace the assembly with their presence—otherwise, probably, Mr. Desmond would not have numbered them amongst his audience.

By degrees, as people came in, and the spaces were filled, Lionel found himself pushed up to the place just behind that occupied by Beatrice; and here he determined to stay. He did not know exactly how it was, but whenever he saw her with Mr. Menteith a sort of protecting instinct seized him, and he could not help watching her, as if he were a kind of guardian over her. Mr. Menteith sat next her, and on her other side was Mr. Ashton, who had managed to secure the seat before Lionel's arrival.

By this time Mr. Desmond had appeared on the platform, and various drawings, maps, and models had been arranged around him. He began lecturing in a

desultory manner, from which it was almost impossible to know what was the
real subject of his discourse, yet gliding
along so fluently and pleasantly that his
hearers could not feel bored.

His chief aim seemed to be, to give
his experiences as a traveller in southern
regions, and, as he said, to describe some
of the wonders that were to be met with
in far-away islands, which had been rarely
visited by civilized beings. He inter-
spersed his sketches of savage life with anec-
dotes of European society, little relevant
to the main subject, but affording relief
to it. He also exhibited his views, which
were spirited and artistic, in illustration
of the places he described; and when, at
the close of the first part of the entertainment, he sang a comic song, in imitation
of a wandering Paddy he had met in some
distant region, few were disposed to com-

plain that it was little to the purpose of the lecture.

Mr. Desmond was certainly either an admirable mimic, or the expression and movements of the poor Paddy were a part of him, for he appeared the character to the life.

He was a good-looking man too, which told in his favour with a considerable portion of his audience. Rather above the middle height, well-proportioned, and framed for activity, with a complexion that had been fair and fresh, and was now ruddy and bronzed, a pair of greenish hazel eyes, twinkling with fun, and a roguish expression about the corners of his somewhat large mouth, Mr. Brian Hope Desmond was far from being destitute of personal attractions. His age was difficult to guess; at the first glance his face looked young, and his thick brown hair and luxuriant whiskers were untouched

by time; but there were crow's feet about
his eyes, and puckers about his mouth,
that seemed to denote him a middle-aged
man. He looked also like one who
had never spared himself, or taken much
thought about health and strength—a
man, in a word, to live a short life
and a merry one, rather than a long and
staid one. When he had retired for a
few minutes' rest, the tongues of his audience were loosed from the silence which
his amusing harangue had enforced, and
there was a general buzz through the hall.
Mr. Menteith did not take advantage of
the murmur around him to speak to
Beatrice—his attention, which had been
fixed upon the lecturer the whole time,
appeared still directed towards the platform, or the wall behind it, upon which
was hung a large panoramic view, re-
presenting a broad stretch of ocean inter-
spersed with various islands, which were

to be described in the second portion of the lecture.

Mr. Ashton, however, did not allow the interval to pass in silence; he had succeeded, at length, after a variety of manœuvres, in drawing Beatrice's attention to the gold links which fastened his wristbands, and which, he now told her, contained hair.

"All of them?" said Beatrice, rather amused for the moment—"and all the same hair?"

"Oh no! not all the same; and only three have hair at all. See, this one is empty," and Mr. Ashton displayed one of his studs to view, showing that there was a place for hair at the back.

"I want to get this filled, to make the set complete."

"A bit of your own hair would answer that purpose," said Beatrice.

"Oh, Miss Clyde! what an idea!—I

hope to get some lady to give me a piece of hers."

"Any lady would be very foolish to give you a piece for such a purpose—only to be placed with the hair of three others. Surely the three did not know the use to which you meant to apply their hair?"

"Ah! they belonged to other days," said Mr. Ashton, with a mock sigh. "Poor things! the chestnut tress belonged to one I have told you about. She's married now, poor creature!—married an old fellow as rich as a Jew."

"I hope she is happy," said Beatrice; "I think you did once tell me something about her."

"She must have been a hypocrite," continued Mr. Ashton, now launched on the full tide of sentimental recollections; "I met her at a country house, after we came from the Crimea. She and I were always together—she was fond of riding, so was

I—she drew, so did I—in fact, we were just
suited. I was positive I was in love—I had
often fancied so before, but this time I was
sure of it, and I wrote and told my mother
that I really must marry. She wrote back
—'My dear Alfred, are you mad?—to marry
in your position, and a girl without a
farthing,' &c. &c. Well, I did not care for
that—I was really in love; when, just upon
my mother's letter, we were ordered to
Malta. I took leave of the girl—we were
alone in a boudoir, where I had often seen
her—well, I can only say that if she did
not love me, she was a consummate coquette.
For three months after we arrived at Malta
I did not look at a woman. I used to
wander on the beach alone—did not care
for even horses and dogs—but at last I was
beginning to get tired, and to wonder
whether it really *was* love, when I saw her
marriage in an English paper. I wrote to

congratulate her, and—well, as you observed, I hope she is happy—that's all."

" By your own account, you did not deserve different treatment," said Beatrice.

" Well, I am not a very constant fellow, I own. I was getting tired, and three months is as long as I have ever yet kept in the same mind. But my time will come, no doubt—too soon for me, perhaps —and I shall know what love is in earnest."

The last words were spoken in an expressive whisper, which almost made Beatrice smile. She had no fear of doing great damage to Mr. Ashton's variable heart.

" I wonder you can talk to such an idiot as that man," said Mr. Menteith, a minute afterwards, when Mr. Ashton's attention had been claimed by one of the girls on his other side—" I could not help hearing part of the conversation, and I never heard such trash in my life."

" Yes, it was trash," said Beatrice, "but he is good-natured and harmless."

" You cannot call it harmless to boast of having the hair of three ladies in his possession ?"

" If women are so foolish," said Beatrice, " they deserve to be exposed."

" It is a singular contrivance for wearing hair," said Mr. Menteith; " I prefer a locket. When I have any hair given *me* I shall wear it in one."

" Next your heart, I suppose," said Beatrice, in a half-mocking tone. She knew that Lionel Constable was behind her, and fancied he must hear much that passed, and she felt impelled to adopt this manner.

" Do not scoff," said Mr. Menteith, " the only hair I shall ever wear *will* be worn next my heart. And, by the way, I observe you never wear a certain chain and locket I know you have—the locket is of curious

Peruvian workmanship—does it not suit your taste?"

" It is handsome," said Beatrice, after a short pause, " but I do not like anything round my throat. I never wear a chain."

" You think it symbolical, perhaps," said Mr. Menteith, in a low voice, yet with such distinct emphasis that Lionel heard as well as Beatrice. " You have had it now for some time," he continued, presently.

" Yes: since last November—I am not likely to forget the time," said Beatrice; " but here is Mr. Desmond again—I do not wish to lose what he is saying."

" He does not speak one word of truth in ten," said Mr. Menteith; " I did not think such absurdities could amuse you."

" I feel bound to listen, at any rate, and something in the man himself interests me."

" I am surprised at that, for to me he looks a regular adventurer, of the vagabond species; however, my attention shall equal yours."

And Mr. Menteith was silent—he did attend most rigorously to Mr. Desmond, and what he heard did not appear altogether agreeable to him.

" Trash ! " he muttered between his teeth, when the lecturer was giving a wonderful account of the inhabitants of the Fow Chow Islands, which he said he had visited when he had been a surgeon on board a man-of-war.

"Ah, boys," continued Mr. Desmond, "she was a clipper, the old Medusa !—but such a captain as we had—he'd have lashed the life out of ye, boys, and no mistake, if ye didn't look sharp, and obey the word! Ah, and it disgusted me; his treatment of one poor imp of a half-starved looking lad —not a stupid lad with his head, but a bungler, d'ye see, with his limbs. Many a kind turn I did for him, for I didn't half

dislike him ; but still what could I do, with
the captain over me, that was worse than a
slave-driver ?—but—why should I harrow
the feelings of the ladies, sweet dears, with
tales like these ?   Bless them, I see the
tears ready to start into their bright eyes—
may they never weep. for sorrows of their
own ! May their eyes never be dimmed,
nor the bloom fade from their cheeks ! And
to set their minds at ease about the lad
I've been mentioning, I may just tell them
that for once in his life he was even with
the hard captain, and that I saw him free
from his clutches before 1 lost sight of him.
Ah, my friends, our lives are like so many
different strings running into one another,
getting into knots and coming loose again ;
who knows whether his thread and mine
will ever cross again ?   There's only one
knot, as I needn't tell the ladies, that can
never be untied.   However, we're getting
too much to the serious view of things, so,

to enliven us a little, I'll give you a song,
which I adapted to the music of the savage
regions I have been describing. You see
the instrument I have here—a sort of banjo
—the nearest approach I can find to the
Fow Chowian Trow-low-koi. So you must
make-believe a little, as the Marchioness
said, and imagine a Fow Chowian chief
before you."

The song began and ended, amidst roars
of laughter, under cover of which Mr. Menteith said to Beatrice,

"I wonder how much longer this per-
formance is to last!—it will be very late
before we reach your father's house—cannot
you avoid going to the Carletons' afterwards ? "

" No," said Beatrice. " not without being
rude. Besides, Miss Constable depends
upon me, and she will be disappointed
if we don't go."

" And is Mr. Desmond to return there?"

asked Mr. Menteith, in whose countenance a struggle between ill-temper and polite deference was very visible.

" I believe so."

The lecture proceeded, and at length concluded, without more words passing between Beatrice and Mr. Menteith. When they were about to depart she turned round to take her cloak from the back of her chair, and in so doing met Lionel's look. He would have offered to put on the cloak for her, but a scarcely perceptible movement showed him that she did not wish him to interfere, and in another moment Mr. Menteith had taken it, and was wrapping it round her. His touch lingered about her so long, that Lionel was once more seized by a desire to knock him down, and he wondered that Beatrice allowed such prolonged attentions.

But she stood motionless as a statue, though he could see that her upper teeth pressed her lovely crimson lower lip till they left a mark there. She suffered Mr. Menteith to draw her arm within his, and pilot her through the room, until they reached the door, when Lionel lost sight of their figures in the crowd.

" Well, and I am sure I have seen that Mr. Menteith before," said Mr. Desmond to Lionel, as they stood in the hall of Mr. Carleton's house—" and I've a pretty good guess where it was I made his acquaintance —only his name bothers me—d'ye happen to know his Christian name ? "

" No," said Lionel, "I have never heard it, but I have no doubt I can find it out for you. Mr. Menteith, however, does not seem to recognise you."

" Doesn't he ? I'm not quite so sure about that. I saw more things from that platform than you think, perhaps. I say, I did that Fow Chow chief pretty well, eh ? Everybody laughed but that fellow Menteith, and I saw a scowl on his face all the time."

" Why should he scowl?"

" Thereby hangs a tale," said Mr. Desmond—" at least I think so. But I am mute. Rattling, jolly dog I may be, but I can hold my tongue when honour commands. However, if you can find out his Christian name I shall be obliged to you. I'll try him presently."

" I will discover it," said Lionel; " I suppose you think a surname is more frequently changed than a Christian name, and you have some particular reason for wishing to know Mr. Menteith's?"

" We shall see," was Mr. Desmond's answer, as he walked towards the drawing-room, where most of the party had assembled. There was a tolerable gathering, now that the officers were added to the guests from Wynthorpe. Lionel, after some time, succeeded in speaking to Beatrice, by whose

chair Mr. Menteith kept vigilant guard:
the question he asked her somewhat surprised her. It was uttered in a low tone,
and was simply this—"Can you tell me
your friend's Christian name?" indicating,
as he spoke, Mr. Menteith, who was just
then replying to an observation of Mrs.
Carleton's.

"It is Stephen," answered Beatrice, with
an astonished look. Lionel half smiled.

"You are surprised, but I cannot explain
now. There are other more important
matters which I wish to discuss with you,
if you will give me an opportunity before
the evening is over."

"Hush!" said Beatrice, with a half-
frightened glance towards Mr. Menteith,
who was returning to her.

"This bondage is insufferable!" muttered
Lionel to himself, as he walked away; "it
must be bondage of some kind, which makes
her act in this manner;" and as the recol-

lection of her former defiant air flashed
across him, and he contrasted it with her
present timid yet forced deference to one
who he had been led to suppose was
almost a stranger to her, his spirit rose indignantly, and he longed to crush beneath
his feet the man who seemed thus to make
her quail before him. Anxious to gain any
further knowledge of him that was possible,
he lost no time in giving Mr. Desmond the
required information about the name, hoping
to elicit from him some revelation touching
his former acquaintance with Mr. Menteith,
but Mr. Desmond only said, " Ah Stephen!
—that answers—he is the man, I am confident, though he wants to shirk me—however, I will challenge him."

"Did you know Mr. Menteith many
years ago?" asked Lionel.

" Did I ? I should think so. But I am
not going to tell what he wishes concealed—
no, no—I will try him, and if he disowns

me, I may seek a little revenge, perhaps, but not in the way he thinks—only a low-born fellow could fear such a thing. He little knows the honour of the Desmonds."

A summons to supper interrupted the conversation, and in the breaking-up of groups which ensued Mr. Desmond managed to approach Mr. Menteith.

" What, my friend!" he exclaimed, " have ye forgotten me? I knew your face the moment I set eyes upon it. Ye've not changed much in that way, however ye may in some respects."

"Excuse me," said Mr. Menteith, drawing back from the *empressé* manner of the other, " I do not remember having had the honour of your acquaintance."

" Ye don't!—then ye've a short memory, or I must have changed more than ye. But there's my name—ye can surely re-call that, man—it's a name I'll never be ashamed of, nor conceal from the world

—Brian Hope Desmond—surely ye've not forgot the sound of it?"

"One meets so many people in passing through life," said Mr. Menteith, "that it is impossible to recollect all the names one has heard. I am sorry I cannot remember yours, and I trust you will excuse me. Possibly we met in society in London—such meetings unfortunately soon fade from the mind of a man of business."

"Ay, we did meet in society in London—but we had an earlier meeting than that. However, I see ye don't care to call back old times, and I'm not the man to force myself on any one's notice—so we'll be strangers, if it pleases ye."

Mr. Desmond spoke with an offended air, in which some feeling of real regret might, however, be traced.

"I am sorry you take the matter so seriously," said Mr. Menteith, blandly; "I

fancy one of us must be mistaken, and
I regret extremely that I cannot satisfy
you, by remembering a person like
yourself."

"Oh, I'm satisfied enough now, whatever ye may be," said Mr. Desmond; "and
I see we are blocking up the way—I beg
the lady's pardon for detaining her;"
and with a bow to Beatrice, he stepped
aside.

During supper, Mr. Desmond was the
chief talker, and his stories caused great
amusement, though even those who were
most inclined to like him were obliged
to own that he drew the long bow rather
freely. He spoke much of various cele-
brated persons he knew in different parts
of the world, and discovered that he
had met, at one time or other, relations
of nearly every one present. He had
just been talking about some member of
the Lyttelton family, whom he had known

in Spain, where he said he had served in the Carlist war, when Mr. Menteith said to Beatrice,

"Happily for him, the Lytteltons do not know enough of their family history to contradict anything Mr. Desmond likes to say. When he claimed acquaintance with me, he went a little too far—I am not so easily imposed upon."

"But I don't see what advantage it would have been to him to have established the fact of a former acquaintance with you," said Beatrice, who had observed the discomposure Mr. Menteith had shown on being addressed by Mr. Desmond.

"Only the advantage of knowing a person connected with one of the best houses in the neighbourhood. Depend upon it, with the slightest encouragement, he would have wormed his way into your father's house, and we should never have been free from him. He is just the kind of adventurer to push his way."

"He is agreeable, at any rate," said Beatrice; "and though I cannot quite believe his stories, they amuse me."

And she turned towards the part of the table where Mr. Desmond was sitting, determined to listen.

"Snakes indeed!" he was saying, in answer to some remark of Jessie Lyttelton's, "I should think there is not a man in the world who has been in more danger from the reptiles than I have; but nothing that I have ever experienced can be compared with what happened to a lady, a friend of mine, at Kilgaum, where I knew your cousin, Colonel Morley —a capital fellow he was!—Fenton Morley, of the Gujapore Irregular Horse—too fond, though, of dashing about in the sun— but such a rider!—I shall never forget once when we were out pig-sticking to-

gether, and he lost a favorite horse—
speared him, after spearing the pig—thrust
on the rebound, ye understand. The poor
beast was game to the last, and started
up with the spear sticking in him, ready
for another chase—but we were obliged
to cut his throat. Poor Fenton was
awfully cut up about it—I wish Landseer
could have been there—it was a fine
subject. I tried my hand at a little sketch
of the thing, but I could not do justice
to man or horse."

"But what about the lady and the
snake?" asked Jessie.

"Oh, I was forgetting—more blame to
me, when a lady was waiting to hear.
Well, two friends of mine, only lately married, were walking home one evening from
my bungalow, where I had given them a
neat little bachelor's dinner. They lived
close by, and had only to walk through the
two compounds. All at once, the lady

stopped, and said—'Herbert, love, do look at my foot!' He stooped down, and there, sure enough, was a big snake, twining itself up, not only round her foot, but her very leg."

"And she was walking on all the time!" exclaimed Jessie.

" Of course she was, until she spoke; and then her husband, restraining feelings you can well imagine, at the danger of his young, lovely bride, told her to stand perfectly still, which she did, whilst he found the creature's head, hit it a knock with his stick, and then untwined the reptile. It was twisted seven times round her leg! Now, that's what I call presence of mind, in a young, delicate girl, too, as she was. But we all know what women are, bless them! I've seen them often in danger by land and sea, the darlings! and they'll hold on where many a brave man gives in."

" Have you been much in India, Mr.

M 2

Desmond?" asked Dora Lyttelton; "is it true that the natives have no gratitude? I have heard that there is not a word in their language to express such a thing."

"They are about as grateful as Europeans," said Mr. Desmond, "which is not saying much. I've experienced gratitude once or twice from native servants myself."

"Ah, but you were there before the mutinies?" said Dora.

"That's true, but still I don't believe that, as far as being ungrateful goes, they can outdo Europeans. From them, indeed, at times, I have experienced the basest ingratitude. One ought to get used to it, as one grows older; but I'm of a sanguine nature, and each fresh proof of the ingratitude of my fellow-creatures gives me a new stab."

Mr. Desmond was silent for an instant, and his eyes wandered towards the spot where Mr. Menteith sat. Whether that gentleman heard his words or not was doubtful : he was busily engaged in helping Beatrice to some jelly, but she fancied that his pale face grew a shade more cadaverous. The Irishman presently continued,

" Now, there's one man of the present day who has been largely accused of ingratitude, and I for my part must say that I consider the accusation false—I allude to the present Emperor of the French. I knew him well when he was in England, and was able perhaps to do him some little services—what they were I forget—I never did, and never could, keep an exact debtor and creditor account of such things. However, let that pass. Soon after he was made emperor I happened to be in Paris, and met him in the street. 'What!' said he, 'Brian Hope Desmond, my boy, is that you? Remember this, my friend, so long as I am Emperor of the French, there will always be a knife and fork for you at the

Tuileries.' I think it my duty to tell this little incident whenever I hear Louis Napoleon's gratitude called in question."

Soon after this anecdote, which seemed the climax of Mr. Desmond's wonderful experiences, the ladies retired. They were soon followed by the gentlemen, Mrs. Carleton having intimated that there would be a little dancing.

As Mr. Menteith only danced quadrilles, Beatrice was free from his attendance during the other dances, and Lionel engaged her for the first waltz. They were waiting to begin when Mr. Desmond came up, and said, in a low tone, to Lionel,

"Did ye see his face when I spoke of ingratitude? He knows me, depend upon it, the hypocrite!"

"Are you sure you ever knew Mr. Menteith before?" asked Beatrice, eagerly and hurriedly.

"As sure as I am that I am Brian Hope

Desmond—but he's a friend of yours? I'll not say a word more about it."

"But—" began Beatrice, and then stopped, confused and blushing.

"No, no," said Mr. Desmond, "I know where to stop. D'ye think I would tell what he wishes concealed? No; let him go his way—win himself riches, and a lovely bride—I shall not interfere—his suspicions wrong me."

Beatrice was about to speak again, but Mr. Menteith hurried up to her, asking her at what time she wished the carriage to be ordered. He looked suspiciously at the trio, and there was something in his glance at Mr. Desmond which caused the latter to turn away with an air of offended dignity. Beatrice answered the question, and then, as the music had begun, waltzed off with Lionel.

CHAPTER VII.

BONDAGE.

"You cannot refuse to answer me now," said Lionel to Beatrice, as they were walking up and down the hall after their dance. "Since that afternoon at Glendale you have never allowed me an opportunity of speaking to you, and you left me then in a state of intolerable suspense."

Beatrice was silent for a few moments, and Lionel thought she slightly trembled; at last, speaking with effort, she said,

"I wish— oh! how I wish you had not said what you did that afternoon!"

"Are you then so displeased to find that I love you? Ah, Beatrice, you must have known it long before"--Lionel's voice sank to a low, impressive whisper, and before Beatrice could again speak he led her to a seat at the end of the hall. She sat down, scarcely knowing what she did, and he placed himself before her.

"Now," he said, "we are free from interruption, and I must demand an explanation. I have a right to it, as every man has, who loves a woman as I love you."

"There is nothing that I can explain," said Beatrice, "I can only beg that you will never again speak as you have just done, and that you will cease to think of me—except as a friend."

"A friend!" exclaimed Lionel; "I know too well that there can be no friendship between you and me. I love you deeply, Miss Clyde, and am anxious to make you my wife, and you try to satisfy me by talking of friendship."

"If you will not be my friend you can be nothing to me," said Beatrice, in a faltering tone, lifting for an instant her eyes to his. One gaze into their dark, mournful depths half maddened Lionel—he bent down and seized her hands in his. "Beatrice, you cannot mean to dismiss me—to say that henceforth we are to be common acquaintances? I will not believe it—you could not look as you do, and feel indifference. You could not have suffered me to hover perpetually about you, and mean to cast me off in the end."

"Why not?" said Beatrice, bitterly; "I have been called a flirt before—you have heard me accused of acting in the same way with others—you should have been warned."

Lionel did not answer her, but his manner showed how greatly her light, scoffing tone pained him. Beatrice saw it, and again she changed—a tender shade drew over her face—her eyes looked deeper than ever—full of tears.

" Pardon me," she said ; " I believe your love is real, and I am sorry for your disappointment."

" But why disappoint me ? You have not been flirting with me—I feel sure of that ; and I cannot but believe that some little real feeling has influenced your behaviour to me. Why cannot we both be happy ? "

" It is impossible ! " said Beatrice, with emphasis.

" Would it be happiness to you ? Only say that, and I can bear anything."

" I cannot—I dare not speak!" said Beatrice, turning away her head, that no secrets might be read in her eyes, and withdrawing her hand from his clasp.

Lionel sat down by her, and was silent for some seconds.

"I cannot bear this uncertainty," he said at last; "you refuse me, and yet you half delight, half agonize me, by betraying—"

"Stop!—do not deceive yourself—I say again that it is impossible for me to think of you."

"But not that you have never thought—"

"You are unfair to draw conclusions—"

"I draw no conclusions; you are, as you have always been, a riddle to me—I have been a fool for trying to solve it, and I am punished. Henceforth I shall believe in all that the revilers of women have ever said."

And Lionel, utterly out of patience, was rising to leave her. A light touch on his arm thrilled through his whole being, and changed the current of his thoughts and feelings.

"Do not judge harshly and unkindly," Beatrice was saying; "I should be miserable if you thought ill of me. I spoke hastily just now. I have been foolish with other people, but with you I never thought of—I would die, rather than grieve you!"

Her face, crimsoned with blushes, was close to Lionel's as she spoke. He was sorely tempted to clasp her in his arms—to take for granted that she loved him; but something in her bearing, though she scarcely shrank before his impassioned gaze, made him hesitate.

"You madden me!" he exclaimed; "I dare not interpret your words as I wish, and yet I cannot think you are only seeking to lure me on—to make me love you more and more passionately against my reason, and almost against my will. Beatrice, if it pains you to see me miserable, why cannot you make me happy, by saying you love me?"

"Because — because — oh! do not ask me—do not increase my wretchedness!"

"You have always suffered from some

mysterious sorrow—is it in any way connected with the reason you reject me?"

"I cannot tell you," said Beatrice; "and
all I could say would make no difference
in your fate and mine."

"You do not know," said Lionel; "try
me, Beatrice—my own, only love!"

"Hush! hush!" faintly murmured Beatrice.

"I will face anything," continued Lionel,
"brave anything to win you—nay, without
winning you, to save you from the unhappiness which seems always hovering
over you; whatever it may be, it could not
but yield to the force of our united love.
Tell me only one thing—say that, had these
circumstances which you hide from me
been different, you would have accepted my
love."

"I cannot say it, for your sake and mine;"
Beatrice spoke slowly, as if the words were
dragged forth with pain.

"I am willing to bear any evil conse-
quences that might ensue—only one little
word, Beatrice—darling!—"

"Stop! this folly must cease!" said Beatrice, half rising from her seat, and then
sinking back again, as if drawn by some
unseen force to the spot where Lionel was.

She could not summon strength to leave
him yet.

He saw her uncertain movements, her
trembling limbs, and marked the momentary
light which his caressing words called into
her eyes.

"Beatrice," he said, lingering fondly on
her name, his voice taking that peculiar
tremulous tone which most men use when
their deepest feelings are touched, "Beatrice, my love does give you some pleasure—
I cannot but feel that it does. Why torture
me longer? Own the truth, I am longing
to hear."

"You do not know what you are

asking," said Beatrice; "and if you knew all, you would blame me perhaps for listening to your words. I am bound—no! I dare not tell you now—but you will know soon enough, and then you will condemn and despise me. I don't know what I ought to say, and what I ought to leave unsaid! If you have any fancies, from my manner, that I—oh! forget them—my brain is in a whirl, and I think I hardly know right from wrong! I can only say, go away, and judge me in future as little harshly as you can. It will be better for us to be apart for a time."

"On your account as well as mine?" asked Lionel eagerly.

"For pity's sake, do not ask me these questions!" said Beatrice imploringly; "I verily believe I shall go mad—and madness scarcely seems an evil now."

And, as if utterly exhausted, she leaned her head against the side of the couch,

with her face hidden under her hands.
There was a step along the hall—
Beatrice recognised the tread, though
Lionel did not, and she raised her head
suddenly, showing a countenance so
scared and bewildered, that the sight
of it harrowed Lionel's heart, and caused
pure pity, for the moment, to overmaster
his great love.

Mr. Menteith approached; he looked
inquisitively at Lionel, but Lionel was not
disconcerted, and spoke first.

"It is pleasantly cool here," he said.
"Mrs. Carleton insists upon making her
drawing-room cheerful with a fire, on
September evenings, but with a large
party the heat is rather superfluous."

"I did not know where Miss Clyde
was," said Mr. Menteith, "and they
are just forming a quadrille. Will you
dance with me?" he added, to Beatrice.

She bowed, got up and took his arm;

but Lionel saw that she walked heavily, and as she turned the corner of the hall, where the passage branched off to the drawing-room, she looked back for an instant. The glance was perhaps involuntary, but once more it seemed to set his brain and heart on fire.

"She loves me!" he thought; "but she is bound—and that fellow is connected with her bondage;" and he recalled the scraps of conversation he had heard between the two at the lecture. He did not stay alone much longer; he returned to the drawing-room, and did his duty, in dancing with various young ladies, carefully avoiding harassing Beatrice by any show of attention, but not one of her slightest movements escaped him.

Mr. Menteith was also observant of her; when not absolutely talking with her, he was never far distant from her, and he listened eagerly for every word that fell from her lips. But Beatrice did not talk much; yet her silence was not the haughty silence of former days, but rather the visible sign of a depressed, crushed spirit, which nothing could rouse.

"Mr. Menteith is a very agreeable man, don't you think so?" said Dora Lyttelton to Lionel, when they were dancing together.

"Yes; he can talk well," answered Lionel.

"It is a pity, though, that he seems so jealously attentive to Miss Clyde," continued Dora; "and she does not half appreciate his devotion. What can have come over her? I never saw her so abstracted before."

"She is tired, perhaps," said Lionel; "are you ready to go on?"

"Miss Clyde is caught at last," remarked Colonel Morley to Mr. Carleton;

"she never looked as she does now, with any of her former adorers. Ashton may hang up his harp on a willow tree, for the twentieth time."

"Do you mean that Mr. Menteith is the favoured one? I give her credit for better taste, myself—indeed, I was beginning to hope that she and Lionel Constable were coming to an understanding."

"Oh, I don't mean to imply that Miss Clyde is in love with Mr. Menteith," said Colonel Morley—"simply, that she will marry him; I would not mind betting a trifle on the subject."

"I would rather not bet about Miss Clyde—or, indeed, about any lady," said Mr. Carleton; "but I really consider your idea somewhat unfounded. Mr. Menteith is almost a stranger to her."

"How do you know that they have not met before? And even if they have not, a few days in the same house do a great deal, and Miss Clyde is quite attractive enough to charm at once."

" I don't dispute that in the least, but I do dispute the fact of her finding anything attractive in him."

" My dear fellow, when do you find men and women equally matched ? Don't you perpetually see fine handsome girls throw themselves away on little snobbish men ; whilst one often knows a famous, genial, open-hearted fellow married to some prudish, egotistical, die-away woman, without a single charm, personal or mental ? Oh, depend upon it, this will be a match—Miss Clyde has just the subdued look of one who has found her fate ; those high-spirited girls always turn the meekest and tamest when their master arrives."

" But such a master ! "

" Why, the man has some cleverness, and is agreeable in his way, though I confess I don't much admire that priggish style of his, myself. Besides, he watches her as stealthily as a cat watches a mouse."

"I observe what you mean," said Mr. Carleton, "and it is positively painful to see a girl like her subject to such scrutiny. I don't know how it is, but that man gives me an antagonistic sensation; he did from the first moment. And I hear he disowned former acquaintance with Mr. Desmond, which looks bad."

"I am not surprised at that, for I should think Mr. Brian Hope Desmond is a man to lay claim to acquaintance which has never existed."

" Oh, of course, I don't pretend to believe all he says, but his manner, when he spoke to and of Mr. Menteith, bore the mark of sincerity. It was quite different from his off-hand boasting style at supper."

" Well, he is an amusing fellow, whatever else he may be; and I have asked him to dine at mess to-morrow."

Meanwhile, Mr. Menteith was making himself agreeable to Mrs. Carleton, and impressing her with the idea that he was an exceedingly gentlemanly and entertaining person. She approved of him more than of the other stranger, Mr. Desmond, whose jokes were becoming rather too much for her to bear, and who indeed, as the evening wore on, did wax a little too emphatic for the company of ladies.

"Do you know how long Mr. Desmond is going to stay in this place?" asked Mr. Menteith.

"No; but I hope not long," returned Mrs. Carleton, "for I am sure he will never be out of this house whilst he stays at Railton. Mr. Carleton likes that sort of people; and indeed he is amusing for a time, but one tires of that sort of thing. He came yesterday afternoon to show us his drawings, and did not leave till one o'clock in the morning. Of course I retired before then. I am

not fond of those artistic, talented people,
and I see far too much of them. I must say
I have a weakness for a little respectability."

"I quite agree with you," said Mr. Menteith, whose attention was wandering towards Beatrice. Lionel Constable was just
then speaking to her, simply delivering a
message from Amy, who wanted her to sing
a duet with her. The mere sound of his
voice, however, caused a start and a blush,
which opened the eyes of Mr. Menteith to
many things. The look of momentary pleasure which came into her face was immediately chased away by a dreary gloom, as
she languidly rose, and moved across the
room to join Amy at the piano.

"I am afraid you will think me a very
strange person, Mr. Menteith," said Mrs.
Carleton, "for talking so freely of one
of my guests—you will suspect me perhaps
of abusing you too behind your back."

"Such birds of passage as Mr. Desmond

and myself should not be too particular as to the criticisms that are passed upon us when we are received upon trust."

"Are you quite a bird of passage, then?" asked Mrs. Carleton, regardless of the fact that Beatrice and Amy were beginning to sing, and not observing that Mr. Menteith wished to listen.

"That depends upon circumstances," he said; "it is a great treat to me, as you may imagine, to stay in an English home, after being in a distant land so many years."

"It must be—and the Palace is such a nice place, and Mrs. Clyde a sweet woman when her health is tolerable; but Miss Clyde is of course the chief attraction. I dare say many people would give a great deal for the chance of staying in the same house with her."

"Has she been very much admired here?"

"Oh, immensely!—indeed, the gentlemen

were wild after her at first. Gradually they cooled, I think, fancying her too great a flirt. But even now she has two devoted slaves, Mr. Constable and Mr. Ashton."

"Ha! and which does she prefer?"

"Why, she cannot care for Mr. Ashton, he is only a boy, and a great noodle; so I suppose Mr. Constable must be the favorite. But really Miss Clyde is a young lady I have never been able to understand, and I ought not to talk in this way to you—no doubt you know more of her than I do. And, after all, I admire her extremely; how splendidly her voice came out just now!"

The song concluded, and Mr. Menteith walked towards the piano; Mr. Desmond and Lionel were standing by it, and the former was saying,

"Bravo! bravo! I'm glad ye sing Irish songs—they are worthy of your sweet voices, ladies. And, by my faith, if Tommy

Moore had not left little to do in that line, I'd try my own hand at composing a stave for such darlings as you."

He slightly tapped Amy's shoulders in his enthusiasm, and she shrank away, over-powered by such vehement admiration. He was just turning to Beatrice, who remained seated on the music-stool, when Lionel quickly placed her arm within his, and drew her towards a seat at some dis-tance.

" Mr. Desmond is becoming rather too demonstrative," he said ; " I thought you did not see him, and I was uncertain what he might do next. "

" Thank you," said Beatrice.

Mr. Menteith, who had seen the whole occurrence, and marked the unmistakeable look of lingering, protecting fondness on Lionel's face, now advanced hastily to Beatrice, and said,

" If I may advise you, Miss Clyde, it

would be well to order the carriage at once—it is time, I think, for the ladies to leave."

"I am ready," said Beatrice; "I will tell Amy," and she went across the room, Mr. Menteith following. Good nights were now said; and she left the room, leaning on Mr. Menteith's arm, Lionel taking care of his sister.

At the door of the carriage Lionel held out his hand to Beatrice; she gave him hers, ungloved; it felt cold, and lay motionless in his grasp; he only kept it an instant, and, with a scarcely audible good night, the two parted.

CHAPTER VIII.

GUESSES AT TRUTH.

THE moment that Amy Constable found herself in the carriage with Beatrice and Mr. Menteith, she felt, not exactly in the well-known situation of being " de trop," but rather as if her presence were acting as a hindrance to some outbreak of hostilities between her companions. An air of heaviness and constraint rested upon the trio. Beatrice leaned back in weary abstraction, and Mr. Menteith, from his seat opposite, as Amy could see by the full moonlight that streamed into the carriage, watched her intently with an expression difficult to read—it might perhaps have indicated love, but for a keen, cruel gleam that occasionally shot from his eyes, and more closely resembled resentment.

At first there was unbroken silence in the carriage, but after some time Mr. Menteith politely addressed himself to Amy. He asked her about her pursuits, her tastes, and her neighbours; and presently she found herself, she knew not how, engaged in giving him descriptions of the different country excursions in which she had lately taken part.

" Indeed ! then your brother and you did this, that, or the other? Miss Clyde was with you there? And Miss Clyde and your brother distanced you all?" Such were some of the leading questions by which Mr. Menteith managed to draw from Amy a pretty correct idea of how

Lionel and Beatrice had been occupied on all these occasions.

At length Beatrice aroused herself.

"Amy, I don't know whether you are aware of it," she said, "but you are being cross-examined. Mr. Menteith has a very inquiring mind, and, never having known anything of village life before, he appears quite attracted by the sort of gossip it affords. You ought to have made up some marvellous story—I assure you he would have swallowed it."

"Truth is sometimes stranger than fiction," said Mr. Menteith.

"That is perfectly true," said Beatrice with emphasis; "perhaps you could relate some stories out of your own experience, Mr. Menteith," she added, in a rather defiant tone, that puzzled Amy—"quite as wonderful as anything we have heard to-night from Mr. Desmond."

Mr. Menteith bit his lips.

"The impertinent fellow!" he exclaimed, "daring to thrust himself into society, and claiming acquaintance with people he knew nothing about. He ought to be exposed as an impostor. I feel sure Miss Constable was grateful to me for proposing to bring you away. I believe that Miss Clyde does not know how to tear herself away from a dance; but for my part, I thought Mr. Desmond's society anything but agreeable for ladies, and I pitied any one upon whom he fastened himself."

"He was very amusing, I thought," said Beatrice.

"And amusement is the chief end of life," said Mr. Menteith; "I remember you expressed this opinion before, Miss Clyde."

"I don't see that amusement is a worse aim than many others," said Beatrice. "It does not injure a person's higher faculties and instincts, more than money-getting, for instance, or ambition of position, reputation,

&c. And everyone has not a vocation for fine feelings and domestic affections, which I suppose are legitimate sources of happiness."

"Happiness and amusement are very different," said Mr. Menteith, in an impatient tone.

"I am quite aware of it," said Beatrice; "the one is more difficult to obtain than the other—and my theory is this, if you cannot be happy, do all you can to be amused."

Her light manner of saying these words did not conceal a good deal of bitterness which lurked in them, and Amy was far from believing that Beatrice really held the theory she professed. It was only assumed, Amy thought, out of a spirit of contradiction to Mr. Menteith, whom this half-cynical tone seemed greatly to annoy. Just then, however, Amy's speculations were interrupted by her becoming aware that the

contempt. It was an immense relief to
Amy when, the Palace being reached,
her companions alighted, and she was left
to pursue her way alone.

Beatrice, on entering the hall, inquired
if her father were up, and, receiving an
answer in the affirmative, she was hurrying towards his study, when Mr. Menteith
seized her cloak, and drew her back into
one of the large recesses formed by the
mullioned windows.

"Let me go!" she exclaimed, indignantly;
"I will call Watson back."

"No—no—you will not make a scene,"
said Mr. Menteith, quietly, as he let her
cloak drop free, and planted himself straight
before her; "I only wish to know if your
behaviour this evening is a sample of what
I am to expect from you? You have
treated me with marked contempt. Your
father, I am sure, would regret that a visitor
—a visitor like me—should be so treated."

"In what way have I failed in polite-
ness?" asked Beatrice, with white lips, and
a suppressed voice.

"You took pains to avoid me whenever
you could—you opposed my opinion by
sneers wherever it was possible."

"Nay," cried Beatrice, "except just
now, I was most deferential."

"Deference is not what I want," said
Mr. Menteith, with a visible effort to master
his passion; "I want the behaviour that you
would display towards a gentleman who is
evidently desirous of pleasing you. You
can show it to others—you listen with
pleasure and answer with animation. With
me, you appear to be undergoing martyr-
dom, and barely to tolerate me. As your
father's guest, I have a right to expect different conduct. You show that you dislike
me in every way—that my conversation is
disagreeable. Everyone is more welcome
than I—chattering boys, with whom I may

surely measure myself as a companion, without losing by the comparison, you honour with attention; and you can even bear the flatteries and the rhodomontade of an adventurer—one who is not even a gentleman, and whom no one knows."

Beatrice looked him full in the face; whatever timid deference had marked her manner at different periods of the evening was gone now, and her eyes shone in the lamp-light with a steady defiant gleam. Her words scarcely seemed an answer to his speech.

"Your hardihood astonishes me," she said; "I am struck dumb with admiration of your talents."

"That is your way," exclaimed Stephen Menteith, a painful quiver distorting his features, as if he were stung; "you delight in sneering at me, but, at least, common courtesy is due to me; and perhaps," he added, raising his voice into the thin shrieking tone he used when excited, "you will find it better not to treat me with either neglect or scorn!"

"I know," she said, calmly; "but I would rather not conciliate. The more you hate me, the better I shall be pleased."

"Hate you!—you little know——" Stephen checked himself, and Beatrice shuddered, as his changed glance fell upon her.

"Yes! you shudder now—you are afraid I shall be too hasty in pouring forth professions unfitting the present footing we are upon. But do not be alarmed. I will not say more than this, that your beauty is dazzling and makes me forget myself, and covet madly the smiles you bestow upon others."

"Let me go to my father!" exclaimed Beatrice, hastily; "I will tell him you insult me by your——"

"He will be on my side," said Stephen; "he watched you the other day, and saw how marked your preference was for another person. Of course I know you are admired, but, Beatrice, no one has admired you as I do—no one sees all in your eyes that I do; yes, you may cast them down— your eyelashes only give me another beauty to contemplate. Miss Clyde, you are adorable enough to tempt a staid man to desperation—but I will be patient."

"You are mad, I think, Mr. Menteith— you strangely forget your present position," said Beatrice, with strong emphasis; "remember this, that so long as I am under my father's roof, I will not be spoken to in this way, even by a favoured guest like you."

Her eyes sparkled, her cheek glowed crimson.

Mr. Menteith's bearing changed; whatever madness had prompted his last speech was vanquished, and his old, studied manner was re-assumed.

"I was forgetting—my courtship is too

sudden, you must excuse a momentary impetuosity—I will restrain my ardour till a more fitting time."

His changed manner seemed to reflect itself upon Beatrice—she grew calm and rigid, only there was a trace of contempt either for herself or him, perhaps for both, in her cool voice, as she said—

"We are as we were, then; and papa will wonder why we are lingering; I am going to say good night to him."

Mr. Menteith followed her into the study where Mr. Clyde was sitting. A few questions and answers ensued about the occurrences of the evening, and then Mr. Menteith looked at Beatrice as if he expected that she would retire. But she lingered, carefully putting aside stray books, and arranging the papers and pamphlets upon the table.

"Well, Beatrice, it is about bed-time, I

think," said Mr. Clyde, at length, and Beatrice started, and said—

"Yes, I must say good night."

Again she looked at Mr. Menteith, as if she thought he ought to go, and leave her alone with her father; but he appeared determined to wait and hear all she had to say. Her lip curled slightly as she went up to Mr. Clyde and said—

"You arranged to go early to-morrow to shoot at Lansdale, did you not?"

"Yes, Beatrice."

"But there is a cricket-match to-morrow in the park at Wynthorpe, and I promised the Lytteltons to go and see it. I want you to put off your shooting and go with me."

Mr. Clyde looked doubtfully at Mr. Menteith.

"Miss Clyde does not consider my escort sufficient protection," said Stephen, in an offended manner.

"Come with me, dear papa," said Beatrice, in an under tone; "you ought to do it, and I don't choose to go about with Mr. Menteith as my sole chaperon; I have had enough of it to-night."

"Well, well, Beatrice, I will go with you," said Mr. Clyde; "perhaps it will be better; people may think it odd, so soon——"

"Such an old friend of the family as I am might surely be trusted," said Mr. Menteith, in a half-ironical tone; "but young ladies cannot be too prudent."

Mr. Clyde did not reply; something in Mr. Menteith's tone or words seemed to affect him, and there was a tremulousness in his "good night" as he pressed Beatrice closely in his arms, and he returned her kiss with more warmth than usual.

She left the room quickly, just offering her hand to Mr. Menteith as she passed him, and snatching it hastily away again.

But the movement was unnecessary, for
this man, a strange mixture of boldness and
bashfulness, had no intention of pressing,
however slightly, the little palm, whose
contact yet communicated an electric thrill
to his frame. He appeared perfectly calm
and grave, and in a half-sullen half-dignified
way, he said, as he held open the door for
Beatrice to pass through—

"You are determined to show me you
resent the boldness of my expressions this
evening, and I submit. I will always for
the present act as if your father were by,
and also leave you to his supervision, since
you appear to consider I interfere in an
unwarrantable manner with your actions."

Beatrice looked at him as if she neither
understood him nor cared to understand,
and then hurried away to her room.

Amy Constable, meantime, had arrived
at her home, and was giving her mother a
description of the evening she had passed.

She was in the midst of one of Mr. Desmond's stories when Lionel entered, and, suddenly breaking off, she dashed at once into an account of her singular drive from Railton.

"Only fancy, Lionel, Miss Clyde insisted on my going round by the Palace! She seemed to dislike being left alone with Mr. Menteith, and they were so disagreeable all the way—at least he was, and she snubbed him so queerly, and yet was afraid of encountering him by herself. I could not understand it."

"I thought he was quite a stranger here," remarked Mrs. Constable; "she can scarcely be intimate enough with him to be afraid of him."

"I don't know; I know he has been away from England for eight years, for I heard him say so; and she does not appear to have known him before. They never refer to the past in any way, and they are very formal, in spite of all this sparring. I feel sure she hates him; and whether he is falling in love with her, and that makes her afraid of being left with him, I can't say. I know I was very glad to get rid of them, and I would never have gone round but for one thing."

Amy checked herself, and began talking of Mr. Desmond again, till her mother insisted on her going to bed.

As she was opening the door of her own room, Lionel touched her on the shoulder, saying—

"You have not kissed me yet, Amy," and he kept her talking for a minute or two. Then, quite abruptly, he said—

"What was it that induced you to go round by the Palace, Amy?"

"Oh! Lionel, it was nothing, really. Only Beatrice seized my hand so eagerly as she begged me to stay, that I could not resist; for you know she is not given to

that kind of thing—I mean hand-clasping,
and whispering, and making things of im-
portance--and I thought she was very much
in earnest; and she looked very unhappy
and very proud. I think it must have been
chiefly to vex Mr. Menteith that she wanted
me to stay, for he looked like a bear afterwards, and gave up being polite to me, and
she went on so."

"Well, good night, Amy," said Lionel,
hastily, and he left her.

Lionel Constable's reflections this night
were not precisely such as properly belonged
to his character as a rejected man. The
more he reconsidered his conversation with
Beatrice, the more attentively he recalled
every circumstance of his intercourse with
her—every sign of hidden sorrow—every
wild and bitter word that had escaped her
—the more firmly he became convinced
that she really loved him. For a brief
period this sweet consciousness filled him

with bliss; if true love existed between him and Beatrice, no obstacle could be powerful enough to part them—his will and energy would overleap every barrier.

But this obstacle, what could it be? It must be of no ordinary nature, or Beatrice would not have shrunk, in such terrible agitation, from declaring her feelings; she had tried to make him believe that it was insurmountable, but that was a notion he would not for an instant entertain.

She was bound, perhaps, by some secret engagement entered into against her will, or formed in some rash moment, and long since repented. Naturally, at this point, Lionel thought of Mr. Menteith; if Beatrice were engaged to anyone, it must be to this man, who seemed to exercise such strange power over her, and to be regarded by her with so much dread and aversion.

The words Lionel had overheard at the lecture certainly indicated that there had been some former intercourse between Beatrice and Mr. Menteith, and yet to the world he had been represented simply as a visitor, who had a share in Mr. Clyde's business, and who had lately returned from South America. He had spent eight years there, and eight years ago Beatrice must have been a mere child, too young to enter into any engagement, and certainly unlikely, at that early age, to be captivated by a man like Mr. Menteith.

Still, allowing that there was an engagement, it might be cast aside; it would be better, both on the grounds of common sense and from higher principles, to break a pledge that could not be honestly fulfilled, than to keep it, and enter into the most sacred of all bonds with a lie upon the lips. Lionel knew well the opinions of Beatrice on this point; she had not hesitated to declare that she would rather draw back from the altar than marry a man she

could not love, for the sake of keeping in
the letter a promise that had been broken
in the spirit.   It was clear, then, that she
did not consider an engagement irrevocable
—the barrier she had mentioned must be
more formidable than this.

Again and again he pondered over every
sentence he could recall, which had implied
that she was chafing under some bitter
bondage—a bondage of long continuance,
since, in the early days of their acquaintance, he had discovered many a mark of
mysterious grief—many an indication of
discord in her noble and generous nature,
scarcely to be accounted for except on the
supposition that some galling, warping influence had been at work; and as he
weighed, with the keen discrimination of a
lawyer, rather than with the anxiety of a
lover, every trifling circumstance, every
doubtful word—as, in particular, he re-
flected upon her behaviour on the day of

Helen Lyttelton's marriage, an idea flashed across his brain, which, if it could be proved correct, would furnish a complete solution to the whole mystery.

But the thought was so wild and impro- bable, that he cast it from him at first, as the product of an excited imagination. Yet it would return, and with such pertina- city, that he could hardly refuse to consider it in the light of an inspiration. The more closely he examined it, the more tenable it became, and it gained at length such form and substance, that he could not rest with- out endeavouring to ascertain, by every possible means, its truth or falsity.

The result of his meditations was a deter- mination to go to London; and at break- fast next morning he told his mother and Amy that he should leave home on the fol- lowing day, private business requiring his presence in town.

He delayed his departure for this one

day, partly because he did not wish to
startle and annoy his mother by leaving her
without warning, partly because he had
remembered the cricket-match in Wynthorpe Park, and he was not unwilling to
see Beatrice once more.

He had no intention of even speaking to
her — no hankering after one of those
strange, regretful glances that filled him
with such painful pleasure; no—so, at
least, he fully believed—his sole purpose in
looking upon her again was one of calm
investigation.

Mrs. Constable and Amy, though per-
plexed by Lionel's announcement, since
business was not rife at this season, concluded, of course, that it was connected
with his profession; and his silent, abstracted
demeanour led to a belief that it was of a
serious, intricate nature.

The cricket-match in Mr. Lyttelton's
park was between the Wynthorpe club and

one of a neighbouring village. It was a purely local affair, and the spectators, though numerous enough, since all ranks were present, were chiefly inhabitants of the immediately adjoining district. There were enough of Beatrice's acquaintances in the field to make Mr. Menteith proud of being able, with the evident good-will of her father, to monopolize the attention of the beauty of the neighbourhood.

She walked up the ground leaning on her father's arm, but with Mr. Menteith on the other side, carrying her parasol, and addressing her repeatedly in a sufficiently *empressé* manner to call forth remark.

"What an awful spoon!" ejaculated a young Lyttelton, who was of an age to despise beauty, women, and lovers. "I wonder a girl does not box a fellow's ears when he looks so soft; but I suppose the noodles like it."

"He does not always look so soft, I can

tell you," said Fred. "I'm sure he gave some savage enough looks last night, both at Miss Clyde and that lecturing fellow."

Lionel was standing with the two brothers, but he did not speak; he did not agree with the younger one in considering Mr. Menteith's manner "spooney;" it struck him as being too terribly earnest to deserve that appellation — indicative, in fact, of a powerful passion, whose manifestations were restrained by the formality habitual to him, and which tinged even his attempts at paying common attentions.

Lionel established himself in the marker's tent, from which, unnoticed, he could keep the benches set apart for the ladies in full view.

He saw that Mr. Menteith seated himself on the grass, at Beatrice's feet, but his attitude, even in that apparently careless position, was stiff and constrained. It was evident that he was desirous of making

himself agreeable to Miss Clyde, and he
made no secret of his pretensions; also, that
he was jealously alive to any interference
with his claims, yet he made no demonstra-
tion of an intimacy, beyond what was war-
ranted by a residence of a few days under
the same roof. Though the night before
something of authority might have been
traced in his air, to-day there was nothing
of the accepted suitor in his manner; he
was neither sentimentally spooney nor
flirtingly gallant; his behaviour was that of
a man who has made up his mind to have
a certain woman for his wife; who systematically conducts his attack, and zealously
watches against the approach of any other
man.

Mr. Clyde lingered near Beatrice, but
not so as to join in the conversation Mr.
Menteith was holding with her. There
were other ladies on the same bench, but
Beatrice sat at the end, and it happened

that those nearest her were enthusiastic girls, who understood cricket as well as their brothers, and were completely absorbed in the game. There was nothing to prevent Beatrice from giving her undivided attention to Mr. Menteith, and yet it scarcely seemed that she did so. Lionel could see that she was very pale, and that there were the dark rings round her eyes, that told of sorrow and sleeplessness.

She appeared to speak rarely, and her glance wandered round the field. Suddenly it fell upon him, as he lay extended within the shadow of the tent, and there came a fugitive light into her eyes. Lionel's blood rushed tumultuously through his veins, for the moment he was tempted to dart towards her, to compel her to own her love, to snatch her to himself, regardless of all hindrances, real and imaginary.

But he restrained himself, he even changed his position so that she could no

longer see him. In a short time Beatrice
also, with the restlessness of misery, changed
her place — the continual sound of Mr.
Menteith's voice in her ear—his well-turned
sentences — and his respectful devotion,
were more than she could bear. She insisted on his taking her to another seat,
where she found herself near Amy Constable, and to Amy she talked with an
almost school-girlish exclusiveness, exces-
sively annoying to Mr. Menteith. Amy, of
course, mentioned Lionel's approaching
departure, an announcement which Mr.
Menteith heard with unmingled satisfaction,
whilst, at the same time, he noticed, with
secret rage, that Beatrice's hand trembled,
and that some of the wild flowers he had
just gathered her, fell, unheeded, to the
ground.

He interrupted the conversation by ques-
tioning Amy about cricket, which she
seemed to understand; and Beatrice, re-

lieved by his addressing another person, turned towards Fred Lyttelton, who was just then standing behind her, and talked with more animation than she had yet shown. Out of pure desperation she forced herself into some display of liveliness, and Mr. Menteith was annoyed by hearing her chat, laugh, and bet gloves, with the young men who, from time to time, came up, during the progress of the game. It appeared to him as if she were determined to show, by the contrast of her manner towards others, with that which she adopted to him, that she only bore with him under protest, and that any respite from his attention and his conversation was grateful.

His vexation reached its climax at luncheon-time. A tent was pitched in the park, and a collation provided by the Lytteltons' hospitality for all comers; but the immediate friends belonging to their own class and set were first marshalled, whilst the rest of the community found places as they could. Mr. Lyttelton, to prevent confusion, had marked off his guests in couples, and, unaware of the true relations between Beatrice and Lionel, and with, indeed, a vague notion that he was doing them a kindness in throwing them together, he had begged Lionel to conduct Miss Clyde to the tent.

Of course opposition was out of the question, and Lionel went up to Beatrice, hardly conscious that a slight emotion of pleasure mingled with his surprise and his sense of the awkwardness of the situation. As he approached, Mr. Menteith was just offering his arm to Beatrice, and she, with an astonished and half-indignant look, made a scarcely perceptible sign to Lionel not to disturb her. He would have retired, but at this moment Mr. Lyttelton's hearty voice sounded at Beatrice's very elbow.

"Come, Miss Clyde, my young gentle-

man is. rather tardy, but you must not
run away without him.   Ah ! here he is—
ready enough in reality, I dare say; but
young men wont appear to jump at
pretty girls, as they did in my days."

The words were accompanied by a
knowing look at Mr. Menteith, as much
as to say,

" Those young people are glad enough
of my help, to bring them together."

Then aloud he said—"I am afraid I
have not set apart a lady for you, Mr.
Menteith—I did not know we should
have the honour of seeing you—but I
hope you will find a comfortable place,
and there are plenty of pretty lasses down
there," pointing to a group of girls who
looked like farmers' daughters, "that
I should have liked a bit of fun with
in my young days, on an occasion like
this. We are very plain people down
here, you see, Mr. Menteith, and it does

us all good to mix together now and then, gentle and simple. It was only because I thought some mammas would be better pleased that I provided partners for my young ladies. But 1 have no doubt that some of my boys and many another will seek theirs down yonder."

"Thank you, I am not a lady's man," said Mr. Menteith, stiffly; "I will look for Mr. Clyde."

"Mr. Clyde is gone in with Mrs. Newton, I believe," said Mr. Lyttelton; "however, don't miss your luncheon, that's all."

"Thank you, I shall do extremely well," returned Mr. Menteith. He was bursting with pride and vexation at being separated from Beatrice—and in such a manner! It would almost have been better if she and Lionel had gone together of their own spontaneous will, and by pre-arrangement! It was so evident that

Mr. Lyttelton thought he was doing them a service! And he had noticed the sympathetic flush of pleasure as their eyes met —he even seemed, by a sort of mysterious *rapport*, to feel himself the thrill that had penetrated Lionel's being, as the light touch of Beatrice's soft fingers rested on his arm.

And to be recommended to find himself a companion amongst the dairy-maid looking girls, whose place was below the salt! A man of standing!—Mr. Clyde's guest!—aspirant for Miss Clyde's hand, as he had determinedly shown himself!—to be exposed to this indignity! —treated like a young, silly boy, or a person of inferior rank! No, indeed; his vanity could not support this thrust! Did he look a likely person so to demean himself?

With an erect air and a slow step, that in a man more favoured by nature might have appeared dignified, but which

in him, with his low stature and insignificant shape, seemed only strutting,
Stephen Menteith walked into the already
crowded tent. Beatrice was seated near
the head of one of the long tables, but
it was quite impossible for him to approach
her, or even to retain a place from which
he could keep her in view.

He was jostled about, nearly knocked
over by impetuous young men, eagerly
rushing to procure lemonade for the
thirsty fair ones, and finally hemmed
in, amidst a group of the girls he had
despised, and the youths of their own
class, or of a higher one, who were paying them attentions, fervid or jesting.
Stephen Menteith hated vulgarity, and
his present society struck him as being
exceedingly vulgar. He could not comprehend young men of any education or
standing lending themselves to the bois-
terous merriment that went forward.

Then one of the cricketers began chaffing him about his absence of mind, in not attending to a request for some of the fowl opposite him for a lady, and his awkwardness in carving it, when he did understand. The girls, too, with all the freedom given by the exceptional nature of the entertainment, laughed at him, and made the young men laugh by their simple witticisms; and Stephen, standing upon his dignity, devoid of the lightness of manner that would have carried him with ease through a situation like the present, only became redder and redder with anger, more and more ludi-crous in his severe majesty.

An occasional glimpse of the back of Beatrice's head—a painful longing to know what she was saying, how she was looking, and how Lionel was daring to behave, combined to render the half-hour within the tent one of the most uncomfortable he had ever passed.

Beatrice and Lionel, meanwhile, had scarcely spoken; if there had been an instantaneous throb of pleasure in their hearts at finding themselves together, it had quickly died away. Lionel respected Beatrice's evident desire for silence and reserve, and sought not to inquire into her wants and wishes, further than as regarded the material affairs of ham, chicken, and sherry; he even turned and spoke to other people, whilst she made flighty attempts at badinage with a cricketing young Lyttelton who was near her; but he could not be blind to the sufferings marked on her brow, the heavy look of her eyes. She could not eat a morsel, the very attempt seemed to choke her; and the observant Mrs. Newton, ever alive to any fluctuation in the complexions and countenances of her neighbours, told her across the table that she looked very ill—probably from the heat, which was unusual for the season, and trying to all who did not enjoy very strong health.

Beatrice replied that she had a head-ache, and that the tent was rather close—she believed she did look pale, whilst even as she spoke a burning flush suffused her face.

At this point, to her relief, and that of Lionel also, the movement of departure commenced; gentlemen and ladies rose from the table together, and once more the tips of Beatrice's fingers touched Lionel's arm. Their progress through the tent was slow; and Lionel, feeling her in the crush pressed more closely to him, could not resist the impulse of protection which prompted him to seek to know and to mitigate her sorrow. Pride — prudence — whatever might have determined his silence — vanished, and, secure from being overheard, as if they had been in a wilderness, he whispered,

" You are ill!—wretched!—I cannot help

seeing it—can nothing be done?—can I do nothing?"

"No—no!" said Beatrice, shrinking as much from him as her position would allow.

"I am not speaking of my love," he said; "I will set that aside and forget it, if on that condition you will let me try to serve you—you *know* this is not impertinence."

"Hush!—hush!" said Beatrice, in a faint tone of real agony, as her fingers closed on his arm with a convulsive pressure, and her eyes rested on a spot near the opening of the tent.

Lionel followed her gaze, and saw Mr. Menteith.

"Confound him!" he muttered involuntarily—"you fear him, then?"

"Oh, hush! hush!" repeated Beatrice, "you are watched—not another word!"

He obeyed her, for her agitation was becoming pitiable—she made, however, a violent effort to master it, and passed Mr.

Menteith with an air of almost indifference. As soon as they were outside, she entreated Lionel to leave her; and he did so at once, returning to his old post in the marker's tent.

Beatrice sat down amongst some ladies, but she could scarcely keep up anything like common attention to what was going on. Her head was throbbing painfully. The heat of the day was indeed unusual for September; there was a heavy mist in the air, and the sun shed a coppery lustre, infinitely more oppressive than the full blaze of golden sunshine. Though the benches were partially shaded by trees, there was a sickly glare, that seemed to penetrate the brain through the eyes; and Beatrice, weak from watching, fasting, and over-wrought feeling, was rapidly succumbing under mere physical pain. She was roused by her father's voice:

" Beatrice, Mr. Menteith is greatly

annoyed," he said in a low tone; "he thinks that you neglect him, and that your behavour is the cause that other people do not treat him with sufficient respect."

"It was not my fault," said Beatrice, languidly; "I did not try to free myself from him."

"Come and walk with me," said her father; "let us meet him, and pray contrive to show a little interest in what he says. He is quite mortified, and inclined to go home; and indeed, Beatrice, it does not look well—no one will suppose——"

"He must be very touchy," said Beatrice; and she rose wearily, and took her father's arm.

Every step she trod increased her pain, but she was too passive to attempt any resistance to Mr. Clyde's will. In a dream-like state she met Mr. Menteith, and found herself soon afterwards consigned to his care. He seemed pacified now—Beatrice release her, and take her to some cool, quiet place?"

"Well, I will do it; she does look ill, no doubt, poor girl!" said Mrs. Constable, more kindly; and, unaccompanied, of course, by Lionel, she went up to Beatrice.

"You are not well, I fear, Miss Clyde," she said; "you will be better in the house—it is so hot here."

Mr. Menteith started to his feet, and seemed to become aware, for the first time, of Beatrice's illness.

"The lady is right," he said; "you are looking ill, where shall I take you?" and he offered his arm.

Beatrice looked appealingly at Mrs. Constable, who said,

"Miss Clyde will go into the house with me; this is the way—follow me."

Mr. Menteith walked slowly, with Beatrice on his arm, guiding her with much

care and tenderness, which she had still
sufficient consciousness to loathe; and it
was intense relief to her, when, at the
entrance of the house, Mrs. Constable dismissed him.

Stephen went away unwillingly enough,
and Beatrice was led by Mrs. Constable into
the little room into which she had been
taken by Lionel, after her wild walk in the
avenue, on the night of the rehearsal. She
did not faint, but she could not repress a
burst of hysterical sobbing; and she then
allowed Mrs. Constable, and the waiting-
maid she had summoned, to lay her on the
couch, and do what they pleased with her.
She remained long in a state of semi-con-
sciousness; not, however, insensible to a
certain soothing pleasure in receiving Mrs.
Constable's cares. That lady's compassion
being now fully roused, she tended Bea-
trie as lovingly as if she had never disap-

proved of her, or suspected her of gaining an influence over her son.

When Beatrice had revived, and the maid had left the room, Mrs. Constable, who could not fail to see that such intense suffering as Beatrice had betrayed did not proceed from physical causes alone, made a slight effort to gain her confidence; but Beatrice did not respond, and Mrs. Constable had too much pride and reserve to repeat the attempt.

"It is nothing," said Beatrice; "I did not sleep last night, and it has been so hot. If I were only at home—don't you think I might go, Mrs. Constable, if I could have the carriage ordered, without saying anything to papa?"

"To be sure, my dear; I will manage that, and let Mr. Clyde know afterwards;" and Mrs. Constable, who had a perfect knowledge of the ways of the house, left the room to give orders.

In a few moments, Beatrice was on her way home, conscious for the present of little save the relief of being alone. Mrs. Constable returned to the cricket-ground to tell Mr. Clyde what had become of his daughter, and met on the way Mr. Menteith, who had been lingering in the flower-garden, and had heard a carriage drive away, without knowing that it contained Beatrice.

He now appeared to much more advantage than he had done in the early part of the day, and, entering into conversation with several people, showed himself what he was — a sensible, well-informed man. Lionel, out of curiosity, contrived to join in a discussion in which Mr. Menteith was taking part, and he could not but own that he spoke well—that his opinions generally had a gentlemanly tone, and that he displayed considerable acquaintance with the world. Still, he remarked a precision of

phrase, and a something stiltified in manner—an overwrought care and watchful-
ness, not usually shown by one whose
station is accurately fixed in society.

Lionel and his mother barely referred to
Beatrice that evening, when they reached
home. Mrs. Constable simply said, in
answer to a question from Amy, that Miss
Clyde had been overcome by the heat, and
had gone home; and neither mother nor
son breathed a suspicion that the pain they
had witnessed had been mental as well as
physical.

Tolerably early the next morning, Lionel
was at Wynthorpe station. He got into an
empty carriage when the train drew up, for
he wished to have, if possible, a solitary
journey, in order that he might, uninter-
ruptedly, re-arrange in his mind the facts
and reasonings which had led him to his
extraordinary conclusion about Beatrice.
It had been neither shaken nor confirmed,

upon the whole, by what he had seen the preceding day; if at one moment he had scouted it as impossible, the next something had occurred to revive his suspicions.

His meditations, however, were not long undisturbed. At the Railton station he perceived a group of well-known figures on the platform, and he was speedily seen and recognised. Mr. Desmond stood in the midst of the circle; he was apparently on the point of starting by the train, and a party of his new friends had accompanied him to see him off.

Mr. Carleton, Colonel Morley, and Mr. Ashton, were present, the two latter looking remarkably pale and "seedy," a condition which was presently accounted for.

"Ah! and so there you are, Mr. Constable!" exclaimed Mr. Desmond, who appeared quite brisk and fresh, and as ready to talk as he had been on the night of the lecture. "It's glad I am to see you, my friend, for I'm feeling quite low-spirited at leaving this place, where I've received so much kindness and hospitality, and met such a set of famous open-hearted fellows, such fine specimens of the British army— connected, too, many of them, with men I'm proud to call my friends. But they'll be hearing, and I scorn to praise people to their faces. So you and I will have a pleasant journey together, I hope — holloa, porter!—if the rascal is not carrying off my portfolio to the van!" and Mr. Desmond rushed away, to look after the safety of his precious drawings.

"He'll talk you to death," said Colonel Morley, during his absence; "he dined with me at mess, last night, and when do you think I got rid of him?"

"Judging from your appearance, not a very long time ago," answered Lionel.

"You're right. How he stands it I can't tell. Would you believe it?—he came to my rooms after we left mess, and he talked to me till half-past seven this morning. Ashton was there, listening to him more attentively than I did. And then, after we had opened the shutters and let in the broad day-light to give him a hint, he said, 'Colonel, I'll just take a snatch of sleep on the sofa there, if I don't inconvenience you— it's not worth while to go to my quarters,' and off he was, as sound as a top, in two minutes; and I verily believe he slept the sleep of innocence till half an hour ago, when he had some breakfast, and went over to Headley's to collect his traps."

Mr. Desmond now re-appeared, and the train being ready to start, he was compelled to abridge his adieux and to jump into the carriage. Lionel's prospect of a quiet journey was annihilated; but he submitted to Mr. Desmond's company with a good grace. He recollected that Mr. Desmond had claimed acquaintance with Mr. Menteith, and he was inclined to believe the claim a just one, in spite of the former gentleman's feats with the long bow; for his manner on the occasion in question had borne every mark of sincerity; and he had withdrawn from Mr. Menteith's notice, like a person hurt and disappointed in feeling, rather than discomfited at failure in imposture. Anything connected with Mr. Menteith was just now matter of intense interest to Lionel, and he trusted to the chances of conversation bringing his name to the surface, and leading Mr. Desmond to say what he really knew of him.

An opportunity soon arose. Mr. Desmond talked of various parts of the world, and the fine fellows he had met in every quarter. He even remembered a Constable he had seen in New Brunswick, and was trying to recollect whether his features resembled Lionel's, when Lionel interrupted him, by saying,

"You have been an immense traveller, Mr. Desmond; may I ask where you formerly knew Mr. Menteith?"

"Ah! that's my secret. He does not wish it to be known; and my honour, sir, never led me to betray what might injure another man, meanly as that man might think of me."

"Excuse my curiosity," said Lionel; "but that seems to imply that you have some secret knowledge which might injure Mr. Menteith."

"I excuse your curiosity easily enough," returned Mr. Desmond. "I can see you are on the look-out for anything about the man who is wanting to snap up the fine young woman he was with the other night. I can scent a little rivalry as soon as any one. Well, good luck to ye—I'd rather you won her than a snob like that."

"But if you know anything seriously against him," began Lionel.

"I know nothing against him that should prevent his making his way in the world with honest men. He's mean and a sneak, to be sure; but the world, sir, pardons those faults. I may know something he would not wish to have told, which, if I published, might harm his schemes; but he little knows me if he thinks I cannot keep my own counsel, when I've kept.it—I'll not say how many years. And he had no cause to suspect his old friend—for a friend I was to him, once upon a time. Confidence is sacred, sir; and the man before you never betrayed it. Stephen Menteith, as he calls himself, may make his mind easy—he is safe for me; and only a suspicious hound as he is would have dreamt that a brave Irishman could blazon forth a secret, he'd vowed to his own honour to keep. I'll not deny, Mr. Constable, that my faith in human nature received a fresh shock when the man —however, I'll say no more—I know you'll

respect my feelings and my silence. Let
him go along in his successful career—my
worst wish is that he may fail in his courting.
I grudge him neither wealth nor position ;
but that splendid girl is a million times too
good for him. May she have a far different
husband ! Did I tell ye she reminded me
of one I knew long years ago ? Donna Iñez
da Silvadora ; she was a beautiful creature—
with that Spanish fire in her eyes, our English and Irish beauties—darlings as they are
—seldom shew. I put aside the Scotch ;
their washy blue, or ashy grey eyes, cannot
speak of love. But Donna Iñez, as I was
saying—sweet creature, she was !—had relations, who would never forgive her for loving
a wild Irishman. A cruel brother, a fierce
hidalgo, six feet two, filled in every vein
with the bluest blood in Spain—hurried her
off to a convent. My fire was up, and I
would have rescued her through blood and
death, but we were under orders to march

—a soldier must not desert his post for private claims. I never saw her more, sir. Her high spirit could not brook discipline and confinement—she died, and a monument within the convent walls is all that tells now of Donna Iñez. May the fate of the fair Beatrice be different !"

Once off in the sentimental vein, Mr. Desmond related numerous adventures which had befallen him, in his relations with the fair sex, and from his conquests, appeared to be a veritable Don Giovanni; still, with all his boasting, there remained a tender deference in his way of considering women, which prevented his revelations from being disgusting. Then he rambled into military subjects, and entered into battles and sieges, modes of attack and defence, with such an air of confidence that Lionel could not presume to dispute what he said, though some of the exploits and manœuvres which were narrated, struck him as being much more like the accounts in Dumas' novels than anything he had heard or read of, as belonging to real life; nautical affairs also claimed some of Mr. Desmond's attention; indeed, he appeared to know something of every profession, and had evidently tried his hand at more than one or two.

It was curious, perhaps, that Lionel still felt inclined to believe in the fact of Mr. Desmond's former acquaintance with Mr. Menteith, but his reliance on this point was so unlike what might have been expected from him, and he could so easily have invented a story about Stephen's misdoings, that Lionel was disposed to think that his silence arose from anything rather than from having nothing to tell.

At a station some miles from London, the travellers parted, Mr. Desmond having to pay a visit in the neighbourhood. He left the train with many expressions of regret

at being compelled to separate from so pleasant an acquaintance as Mr. Constable, and
many hopes of a future meeting.

CHAPTER IX.

TWO NAMES.

In a dingy office, looking into a gloomy London street, Lionel Constable was earnestly poring over a much worn and dirty volume, bound in calf-skin. By his side stood a tall, thin, smoke-dried man, who was helping him in his search for an entry he half expected, yet did not wish, to find.

"This book is of too late date," said Lionel; "the one I want to look at is the book that was kept when Mr. Cartwright was Registrar."

"Ah! he was the last Registrar but one

before me," returned the man; "let me see,
185— was his last year — perhaps this
volume will do? or would you like to look
at an earlier one?"

"No! this will do—185— that is eight
years ago," said Lionel, half to himself, and
seizing the book he opened it at the first
page, and began turning over the leaves
carefully.   He was so absorbed in his
object, that he seemed quite to forget the
presence of the Registrar. His tall figure
was bent, his brow contracted into lines of
earnest thought, and his lips, usually expressive of genial, light-hearted enjoyment,
were rigidly pressed together.

Leaf after leaf was turned, but he did
not find what he sought, yet the entries for
half the year had been passed; something
like a gleam of hope arose in Lionel's eyes,
and he scanned the pages with still closer
attention.

July was turned over, but the entry did

not appear—August—then September—first—second—third—fourth—fifth—sixth—the last date on the page.

Opposite this, two names flashed on Lionel's eyes—Stephen Menteith and Beatrice Clyde. There were other signatures, but Lionel saw only these two, standing out clear and distinct from the paper—every turn or flourish in every letter seemed burnt into his brain, never after to be effaced.

"You have found what you wished?" inquired the Registrar, observing Lionel's long pause and steady gaze.

"What I sought—yes," answered Lionel, rousing himself and closing the book; "the sixth of September, eight years ago," he repeated, half to himself, as if to impress the fact upon his mind. Then collecting his self-possession, he went through the formula of offering thanks and apologies to the Registrar, took leave, and departed to his own chambers.

Lionel Constable was now, for the first time in his life, thoroughly miserable. He loved, passionately and devotedly, a woman who could never be his wife—who was the wife of another man—had been his wife for eight years. There was madness in the thought, in the certainty of what had only been a dim possibility—an idea too wild to be really credited.

Beatrice, whom he had believed attached to himself—Beatrice, whose eyes, at any rate, had spoken her love for him—was a married woman—one whom it was now sin to love.

The cause of concealment Lionel could not guess; certain it was that, although passing in the world as Miss Clyde, an unmarried girl, free to receive admiration and love, Beatrice had, eight years ago, been married at a Register Office to Stephen Mentcith, the man who was now jealously watching her, who evidently loved her, and who was now probably about to claim her openly as his wife.

As Lionel contemplated the deception to which Beatrice had lent herself, he could only condemn her—every tender impulse was quenched within him, burnt up in the fire of just indignation. Had she not acted as the freest of the free?—accepted the homage of any man who would offer it?—led on her admirers to speak of love which she could not return, and which, felt for her, was criminal?

All the purity with which he had invested her vanished—she was worse than the most censorious of her critics had deemed her—she was not only a flirt, but a deceitful, unprincipled woman—one without any sense of shame or delicacy. Bound by the strictest ties, she had allowed herself a freedom of action which would have been censurable, perhaps, in an unmarried girl, but which, in her, a married woman, was positively sinful.

Married!—the wife of Stephen Menteith! —loved by him! The images called up by these ideas were terrible. Beatrice, who, he had hoped, was his own Beatrice! Beatrice, who had looked on him with those lingering, loving eyes!

At least, she must have been an unwilling wife; she had been miserable for long; doubtless she felt her fetters a heavy burden; probably hated the man who had imposed them on her. For a moment, Lionel rejoiced in this thought—that she hated her husband—she was his own then still, in feeling, in soul, though she might be legally the wife of Stephen Menteith. *He* could not command her love—that was still his—Lionel's.

But the flash of exultation died out, and left a deeper gloom behind. If Beatrice loved him, the case, so far from being improved, was worse—two, instead of one, were indulging a feeling that was guilty. Yet could that be guilty which was so natural? Married when but a child—probably against her own wish—though whose purpose, except the bridegroom's, the match would serve, Lionel could not guess. Separated, so at least he believed, for eight years, was it likely that she should remain faithful to the remembrance of her scarcely-known husband? Was it natural that all the hopes and feelings of youth should be dead within her—that she should go into society, meet men who were more likely to attract her than Stephen Menteith, and in whom she was more likely to find sympathies and congenial tastes, and yet be able to fence herself round perpetually with the sense of her true position?

The more Lionel thought, the more his first harshness died away; the more he threw himself into her situation, the more excuses he found for all those inconsistencies in her conduct, which had made her a puzzle, not only to himself, but to the whole neighbourhood; which had made him strive not to love her, and yet had added piquancy to the charm that drove him on. All her cynical speeches; her light scoffing at love and matrimony; her wild flashes of reckless mirth, her very coquetries—playing with the shadow, the reality of which she could not enjoy; her unaccountable agitation on various occasions—all gained now their true, their most sad interpretation.

Lionel had gone to London filled with the idea that Beatrice had been married to Mr. Menteith ; and yet he had almost laughed at himself for a notion so far-fetched, and the truth had fallen upon him with a force nearly as overwhelming as if it had never been anticipated. The recollection of Beatrice's visible and uncalled-for emotion when Mrs. Collingwood had

spoken of register marriages, and introduced the name of her late husband—
Beatrice's after-inquiry about Mr. Cartwright, and the whole of her flighty demeanour during that evening, had given
Lionel a clue, which he had determined to
follow, though hoping to find himself under
a delusion. The conduct, indeed, of Mr.
Menteith, and of Beatrice's parents, he had
been unable to understand, on the supposition of such a marriage. Why it should
still be kept secret—why Mr. Menteith
should suddenly appear on the scene almost
as a stranger, and begin, in a matter-of-fact,
purpose-like manner, the wooing of the
woman who was already his wife—were
questions to which he could give no answer.
But, in spite of all improbabilities, he had
felt convinced that some tie of a more binding nature than a mere engagement existed
between Beatrice and Mr. Menteith; and
vague as his ideas were, he had resolved to

test them. Hence his journey to London, and his visit to the Register Office of St. Benedict's, of which the result has been seen.

Beatrice the wife of Stephen Menteith! This thought seemed perpetually present to Lionel's mind, whilst those two fatal signatures appeared to flash for ever before his eyes. A barrier—insurmountable, indeed —as she herself had said, was raised between Beatrice and himself, and bitter separation was to be the only end of the devoted love he had felt, and which she, he fully believed, had been inclined to feel. Separation, endless separation, was inevitable. Lionel would not, dared not, trust himself to see her again. On the day after his conjecture had taken shape he had broken his resolution and spoken to her, forgetful of the dark shadow between them, of which he had caught a glimpse. And now, when dread had become certainty, if

he were to see her with Stephen Menteith,
her husband, the sight would drive him
mad; and if he were to see her alone, to
behold her trembling, suffering—her large
dark eyes melting with regretful tenderness, or wearily cast down in mute agony
—no! he dared not pursue the thought
even. They must be parted—at any rate,
till time had calmed his sensations, and he
had grown accustomed to the consideration
of her as she really was—a woman separated from him by the vows she had taken
with another, not a girl free to be loved
and won.

So Lionel remained in town, finding
work for himself, and labouring manfully
at it; writing home to his mother that he
could not return to Wynthorpe at present;
struggling on through many hours of
despondency, many of fierce passion, of
wild longing and desperation, but presenting to the world a calm, serene aspect, and

showing himself to his friends the genial, generous-spirited, open-hearted companion they had ever found him.

Disappointment could never really sour a nature like Lionel's; it might perhaps sober his views of life—it might cross his brow with a deeper wrinkle, and make his solitary hours seasons of harder discipline and sterner thought, but it could not warp his judgment, or freeze the kindly current of his social charity.

One morning, when he had been about a month in town, a letter he received from Amy revived in their first intensity his feelings about Beatrice. Amy wrote, after some domestic news, the following:

"I think you will be surprised to hear that Miss Clyde is really engaged to Mr. Menteith. I don't like the affair myself, as you may suppose, from what I told you about my drive home with the two from Railton, and mamma says she is sure Miss

Clyde feels no real affection for Mr. Menteith. I fancy mamma found something out
that day of the cricket-match, when Beatrice was taken ill—by-the-way, she was
not well for some days after that, and she
does not look at all as she used to do now.
I don't think Mr. Menteith is half good
enough for her, but every one here almost
has taken to him lately; he has made himself so agreeable, except when engaged in
making love. You know before you left he
was very attentive—well, now he is the most
devoted lover I ever saw—Tom Heywood
was nothing to him; but I cannot think
Beatrice appreciates his devotion, she looks
so unhappy. She came the other morning,
looking like a ghost, and I am sure her eyes
were full of tears, as she was looking at
mamma's flowers. I wish you would come
soon—I never knew you so busy before at
this time of year, and there are several
parties going on, in honour of the Hey-

woods, who returned from their tour some time ago, and are regular turtle-doves," &c.

The picture of Beatrice, pale, tearful, and unhappy—receiving, as a victim, hateful attentions and demonstrations of love—sent a keen pang through Lionel's breast. She was now outwardly engaged; in a short time she would be known to the world as, what in reality she was even now, the wife of Mr. Menteith!

CHAPTER X.

A CHAIN TO WEAR.

BEATRICE CLYDE sat before her dressing-table one October evening; she was dressed for dinner, and held in her hand a small gold chain, with a locket attached to it, of massive, curious workmanship. Her face was working with many strange emotions as she regarded it, and she seemed unable to make up her mind to wear it. In fact, Beatrice could not help considering it as an outer mark of that bondage which was eating into her heart, and which was a strong reality, incapable of being made greater or

smaller by any external sign. Yet, knowing this, she shrank from the symbol; and
she was still turning it over and over in
her hand, when her mother entered the
room.

"Beatrice! not ready yet? Mr Menteith has arrived, and evidently expected
you to meet him. He has gone to dress
now, and you must be in the drawing-room
before he comes down. Ah! you have
taken out the *negligée ;* let me clasp it round
your neck."

"If you like, mamma—I cannot."

"Silly child! I would not quarrel with a
beautiful ornament like that, at any rate,"
and Mrs. Clyde proceeded to put it round
her daughter's throat. Though it hung
loosely from her neck, the circlet seemed to
choke Beatrice, and she shivered at the cold
touch of the gold.

"My dear, it is most becoming," said
Mrs. Clyde, standing a little way off, and

surveying her daughter's queenly head and neck; "do look at yourself. Nay, Beatrice, there is no occasion to look so disdainful. When all is said and done—the man has some advantages, and he is certainly devotedly attached to you. He will lavish treasures upon you; and he will have treasures to lavish, for your father says he is just the man to make a splendid fortune in a few years; and then, you know, you can both return to England, and we can all be happy together."

"Mamma, how can you talk so?" said Beatrice, reproachfully; "you, who talked so differently a short time ago, and regretted so often that I was chained to a man so unlike the husband you would have chosen for me."

" I own I did grumble, Beatrice; but I did not think Mr. Menteith would have altered so much as he has done. I only thought of him as a puny, red-haired

freckled, awkward young man. It is true,
he has red hair still, and it grieves me that
a child of mine should marry a man with
red hair; and no doubt he is far from
handsome, but although looks go a great
way with me, they are not everything;
and he is altogether such a superior person,
and so fond of you, that I really think
you might reconcile yourself to what must
be."

"Fond of me!" exclaimed Beatrice,
stamping her foot on the ground; "that is
just what makes my lot unendurable; if we
had a sort of civil hatred for each other, I
can imagine vegetating on, from day to day,
without coming to any wretchedness greater
than I have hitherto borne. But to be
loved by *him*—by a man I loathe—though
I must call him *my husband*—to know myself bound to submit to his love, and its
hateful demonstrations—to have him imploring, pining for mine; exacting from me

marks of affection and tenderness—jealously watching me—grudging even you and my father the love I give you, longing to merge it all in one large stream of affection for him alone—it is agonizing, mother—my spirit rises against it, and yet I feel powerless. If you knew the relief of these few days without him !—how I have dreaded his return—how I shrink from meeting him to-night !"

"Well, well," said Mrs. Clyde, "you will not see much of him to-night; at a large dinner-party he cannot devote himself entirely to you."

"But he will watch me, and I shall be exposed to the comments of others."

"You used not to care for them, Beatrice."

"No ; but I do now—I cannot bear people to think—at least, the people I care about—that I love Mr. Menteith, nor yet that I wish to marry without love."

"Well, you don't show him much love at

present, certainly," said Mrs. Clyde; "and, after all, I do feel for you—you have not been allowed to choose for yourself, and you have been thrown in the way of others you might have chosen."

"It is not the choosing," said Beatrice, "I suppose few women can really choose; but they may refuse, and I—I have never known freedom, at least since I could tell the value of it—oh! even to feel it for a few moments must be bliss; not to be dragged down by a perpetual weight, crushing all one's desires and feelings; binding even one's thoughts," and Beatrice put her hand to the chain round her neck, as if she would have torn it off, and dashed it to the ground.

"Compose yourself, darling," said Mrs. Clyde, coaxingly; "you really must go downstairs now, and it is no use talking in that way."

"I know it," said Beatrice; "and I know,

also, that I have brought some of my misery
upon myself—I have been deceitful and
wilful, and I ought to consider my unhappiness as only what I deserve. If Mr.
Menteith had come a year ago I should, at
least, have suffered less self-reproach than I
do now."

"Nonsense, child, you have behaved
beautifully, under the circumstances ; if
people choose to fall in love with you, you
could not help it—how could you go and
tell the truth to every man who came near
you ?"

"It ought to have been told," said Beatrice ; "I have been in a false position all
along. I might not be able to remedy that,
but I might have acted very differently
from the way I have done. My reckless
impatience of my fate urged me on."

"But your fate was an excuse," said
Mrs. Clyde ; "though I don't think it is so
very bad, now the time has come ; however,

come along, and don't try Mr. Menteith's patience too much, when he is anxious to see you. It is all very well to spur men on sometimes, but he does not require it."

"Unhappily not," said Beatrice, with a deep sigh, as she followed her mother out of the room.

Mr. Menteith was waiting for them in the drawing-room, and he advanced and met Beatrice with great *empressement*, to which she passively submitted. Mrs. Clyde speedily vanished, to Beatrice's dismay, and she found herself once more face to face with the man who was her husband.

He looked at her for some moments, standing exactly opposite the couch on which she had placed herself.

"You greet me as coldly as ever," he said presently; "no one would think there was any tie between us."

"But since the tie does exist," said Beatrice, "the greeting can be of no great importance."

" It is of inportance," he said vehemently, fixing upon her his small cold gray eyes, lighted now by a look beneath which Beatrice almost quailed; " it is of importance," he repeated, "love like that I feel for you will only be satisfied with corresponding love—the outer tie is nothing to me, if the inner one be wanting."

"Then why," said Beatrice, collecting her courage, "why not break the outer tie? The inner one can never be—no, never!—if we were both to live till doomsday. Why persevere in keeping me thus outwardly fettered, if you do not care for making me simply a slave?" and again, as she spoke, her fingers played half unconsciously with the chain on her neck.

Stephen Menteith changed colour; he grew almost livid as he listened to her; and when he answered, he spoke hurriedly and confusedly.

"What do you mean?—what can break the bond? You are mine, are you not, by law? Who has been filling your mind with these——" he stopped, but soon continued—"what makes you think the knot can be untied? It cannot—shall not be untied! I will declare before the whole world that by the laws of the land I am your husband, and defy anyone to prove the contrary. You do not mean to deny it, I hope?" and he looked anxiously, inquiringly, in her face.

"I do not mean to deny it," said Beatrice; "unhappily, I know it too well; but there might be a separation—if the outward union is worthless to you, we might agree to live apart—such a lot would be comparative bliss to me."

A look of relief came into Stephen's face.

"Oh, that was what you meant!—but that I will never consent to. You shall be mine in name now—I will live in the hope that some day you will be mine in love also."

And again his eyes were fixed upon her with the intense gaze which thrilled her with nameless terror.

There was a short silence. during which Mr. Menteith's glance wandered from Beatrice's face to her neck, and he perceived the chain and locket she was wearing.

"I see you have condescended at length to wear the ornament I sent you," he said.

"You wished it, and my mother wished it," said Beatrice; "and as it is no longer possible for me to deceive myself, or to forget my real position—the wearing of this mark of bondage cannot much signify."

"Take it off, if you can only consider it a mark of bondage," said Stephen, his pale complexion flushing a dingy red, and his whole face working with passion and pain.

"I may as well wear it, now I have begun to do so," said Beatrice; "it is usual for engaged people to wear some symbol of that kind, and I may as well conform to the ordinary rules, since I am to appear as your *fiançée.*"

"I believe you are doing your uttermost to try me," said Stephen, impatiently; but instantly checking himself—"at least tell me one thing," he continued. "Have you kept my hair at the back of the locket?"

"I have never opened it," said Beatrice; "what the locket contains is a matter of indifference to me—to know that it came from you is sufficient."

"Sufficient to make it hateful to you," said Stephen, with an accent of bitter regret; "well, another man might be thoroughly discouraged, but, as your favourite Tennyson says—

'My faith is large in time.'

And the day may come when you will value a lock of my hair, though it is neither raven black like your own, nor fair and golden like——you need not start, I am not going to betray any jealousy, or to blame you for what is past; I have heard some things, it is true, and I may think that, under the circumstances, you might have had the good taste to avoid being remarked upon; but I will not believe that *my wife* could really forget she was my wife."

"Your wife!—no, I feel it too bitterly.   I have tried to forget, I own—I have longed to wake, and find all the past a horrid dream—I have imagined release—oh! if you had a spark of generosity, you would release me!"

"You talk as if release were possible," said Stephen, fastening his eyes upon her; "do you not know enough of the laws of marriage to be aware that nothing can free you?"

"Yes, yes; I know I cannot be really free, but—however, you have answered this before, and it is folly to try to work upon your compassion."

"It is, indeed; love is too strong within me for anything so tame and mild as compassion to exist. Oh! Beatrice, you do not know the love I feel for you—you fascinate me—I can no more help giving myself up to your influence, than I can live without breathing. Is it likely that I can consent to give up the right I have over you? You are mine—you shall be mine, and I will compel your love!"

"Your feeling for me cannot be of long standing," said Beatrice, half shrinking from his passionate words; "when we parted, you knew too little of me to care anything——"

"I did not care, I acknowledge; and, perhaps, I pay the penalty of my carelessness now. Had I cared, I should probably

have used greater efforts to keep my memory
before you, to make you wish for my return.
No, I was content then with the idea of a
wife who did not love me—now, I would
give worlds to gain her love. From the
very first evening of my return I have
worshipped you, Beatrice—I have adored
your beauty, and gloried in knowing that
you belonged to me—more than that, I
have——"

The voice of Mrs. Clyde was heard speaking to her husband in the ante-room, and
Mr. Menteith checked himself, adding only,

"It is sufficient proof of my love, I think,
that it can make me talk in this way; a
staid, business man, such as I am, must
be strangely affected, to fall into rhapso-
dies."

Mr. and Mrs. Clyde entered the room,
and directly afterwards the guests began to
arrive. The party was given partly to introduce Mr. Menteith to the neighbourhood

as Beatrice's future husband; partly in honour of the newly-married couple—Mr. and Mrs. Heywood.

Mr. Menteith had already made a favourable impression, but still his engagement with Beatrice was looked upon with surprise. The affair had been so sudden, and Miss Clyde's former admirers had been men of such a different stamp to Mr. Menteith, that he was not generally supposed to be a kind of person likely to attract her. How they would behave to each other, under their new relations, was a matter of much curiosity, particularly amongst the younger members of the party, who, having lost the opportunity of contemplating the Heywoods in their betrothed state, were not sorry to have another engaged pair brought under their notice.

Stephen Menteith was certainly devoted enough as a lover to satisfy the most exacting of young ladies; but there was something, as Jessie Lyttelton expressed it, " rather stiff and stiltified about his attentions."

It was not that he harassed Beatrice by attempting to keep her conversation to himself, or that he pestered her with secret glances; but he was too solicitous about her, would not allow another person to do anything for her—waited upon her, in short, like a slave. Yet with all this deference a kind of authority was mingled. Beatrice could feel, and others could perceive, that he exercised a right over her, of which he was jealous, and which he seemed frightened of losing, or of letting her forget. As for Beatrice, she reminded people, in a considerable degree, of what she had been on her first arrival at Wynthorpe, before she had adopted what some called her flirting manners. She was cold and uninterested, spoke little to anyone, and very little indeed to her lover; but she bore his attentions patiently, and appeared to yield to his wishes whenever he expressed any. Few could think she was happy, and very little penetration was needed to discover that she was simply passive and resigned with regard to Mr. Menteith; and it was the perception of this that galled him.

It hurt his deepest feelings to see so plainly that he was not loved; and it piqued his vanity no less to be aware that this want of love was manifest to the world.

The contrast, too, presented by the bearing of Mr. and Mrs. Heywood to each other, was very striking. They were in the first stage of honeymoon fondness, and though sensible enough in most respects, they behaved just now as foolishly as the most weak-minded couple in existence. Stephen Menteith, at any other time, would have despised them; but at present he felt that, to be looked at by Beatrice as Mr. Heywood was by his wife, would be the height of happiness.

Beatrice viewed matters differently, and was inclined to be contemptuous, when, after dinner, in the drawing-room, Mrs. Heywood was describing some of her new occupations—revealing how entirely she was moulding her tastes to her husband's—how his pleasures were her pleasures.

Yet a sense of pain mingled with the scene, and Beatrice checked the words that rose to her lips. Helen Heywood had married the man she loved. It might be she did feel all the happiness her speeches and manners implied, although Beatrice could not imagine that she herself could, under any circumstances, speak in exactly the same way.

"Have you heard from Lionel lately?" asked Mr. Carleton, approaching Amy Constable, who, with a few of the junior members of Wynthorpe society, had been invited to join the party in the evening.

"I heard this morning," returned Amy; " he is very busy, he says."

" He is not generally so busy at this season," said Mr. Carleton. " We all depended upon having him here—he stayed much longer last year."

" Yes; that was the time when we were so gay—and there were the charades," said Amy.

"Ah! and the races, too; but that was before he came. We seem to have gone off since last year. Captain Denbigh was the great leader of the fun in those days."

" Were you at the charades they are speaking of?" said Mr. Menteith, in a low voice to Beatrice, who was sitting near Amy. He had been listening to the short preceding dialogue rather earnestly.

"Oh, yes!" said Beatrice. "I went to everything."

"Miss Clyde was a principal performer," said Mr. Carleton. "I shall never forget that scene with the ring — it was so good!"

"Oh! when Captain Denbigh gave the ring," said Amy—"Dear me!—what a pity he is not here now! I was quite sorry when he left."

She stopped suddenly, and coloured slightly, glancing at Beatrice.

But Beatrice was unmoved and colour-less—regardless, apparently, both of Amy's looks and Mr. Menteith's. She said something presently about music, and Amy was asked to sing. Afterwards Beatrice went to the piano herself, and was immediately fol-lowed by Mr. Menteith.

"Of all the jealous people I have ever seen, that man is the worst," said Mr. Carleton to Colonel Morley. "How Miss Clyde endures him, I cannot conceive."

"I was right, you see, in thinking they

meant something serious," said Colonel Morley.

"So you were, I am sorry to say, but I cannot understand it—the girl looks positively miserable."

"She looks as I should not like the girl I was going to marry to look; but, indeed, Miss Clyde has always struck me as an uncomfortable kind of woman for a wife—too much *diable* about her—I could fancy her *strychnining* a fellow to get him out of the way. I beg your pardon, Carleton; I know you and she are great friends, and really, as far as looks go, I have an intense admiration for her, but she is not my ideal of a wife—tender, and gentle, and forbearing, you know—one expects such things in women."

"I don't believe she is deficient in any womanly virtue," said Mr. Carleton, "but I do believe she will be quite embittered and spoilt if she marries that man. I cannot think she has accepted him of her own free will, and he looks as uncomfortable as he can look in his position. And she seems half scornful, half frightened—I should not be surprised if she did not marry him after all."

"I think she will," said Colonel Morley; "but they will lead a cat-and-dog life afterwards."

Mr. Menteith, meanwhile, was trying to have a few words with Beatrice at the piano.

"From all I hear," he said, "you used to be the gayest of the gay—how is it you are so much the reverse now?"

"You know the reason," said Beatrice, "we have discussed it sufficiently."

"But for my sake, for your own sake, you might appear a little more cheerful in society," said Stephen; "I am quite sure people are making remarks upon the alteration in you."

" They are at liberty to do so," said Beatrice, " I cannot undertake to smirk and smile, like Mrs. Heywood, every time you look at me."

" You need not show positive hatred, though," said Mr. Menteith ; " you treat me like a slave."

" I do not intend to do so," she retorted; " I feel too keenly that I am a slave myself."

Stephen Menteith's lips grew pale with repressed passion.

" Are you aware," he said, in a low voice, " that I have still the power to bring misery upon you and your family? If you try me too far, I may use it."

" You cannot, after the contract that has been made," said Beatrice, " unless,"—she looked up eagerly—" unless you could first free me—can you do that?"

" No, of course not," said Stephen—" *that* can never be done—I only spoke to try you," he added, rather hurriedly; "if you were free, and I required again the same condition for my secrecy, would you grant it?"

"No, never!" said Beatrice, with emphasis. "I am a woman now, and I know better how far self-sacrifice ought to go. I know too well that I have condemned myself to wretchedness and to sin—for it is sin to feel as I do—to hate as strongly as I am compelled to do."

"Beatrice, my love," was heard from the other end of the room, in the soft tones of Mrs. Clyde, "will you sing ' The Power of Love,' Mrs. Carleton wishes to hear it?"

Beatrice complied; she sang with as much clearness and expression as ever, whilst Stephen sat behind her, knitting his brows and compressing his lips, feeling, with all his heart and soul, that Beatrice had within her all the passion and tenderness necessary to experience the strongest

form of the love whose power she was
singing with an intensity that could not
have been inspired by the vapid words
alone.   And yet she did not—perhaps
never *would* love him.   How should he
compel her?   He had spoken confidently,
but he now began to feel how powerless
he really was;—a glance in an opposite
mirror did not tend to reassure him—singularly impressionable with regard to appearance as most plain people are.

"All women are alike," he thought; "she
is her mother's own child.   Long, straight
legs, a curly head, and large, languishing
eyes would speak more for my cause than
all the brains I possess, and all the use I
have made of them."

"This is very stupid work," remarked
Beatrice, when she had finished singing;
"no one talks, and everyone looks at everyone else—something ought to be done."

"You are so restless," said Mr. Menteith; " I daresay they are all satisfied, and if they are not, they will only leave earlier."

" You seemed anxious a short time ago," said Beatrice, " that I should appear cheerful, and I have come round to your way of thinking, so far as to wish to keep up my credit as the daughter of the house, as long as I am known as Miss Clyde."

" And after that, will you always be as fond of society as you are now, and seek to shine in it ? " asked Mr. Menteith.

" I don't know—I cannot answer for anything; but society would certainly be better than solitude."

" I cannot wonder at your taste, when you are so fitted to adorn it," said Mr. Menteith ; "and it will delight me to see you admired ; but—" his voice sank lower—" the life I have pictured myself passing with you is very different from a social whirl. Oh ! Beatrice, surely it will be realized some day," and he drew his chair slightly forward, so as to place himself between her and the rest of the party.

"We cannot discuss the question now," said Beatrice; "if it concerns an affair of obedience, I shall submit, of course—if you desire me to spend my life in a *tête-à-tête* with you, I shall not outwardly rebel. A little suffering more or less will not signify. But now you must not hinder my attempt to make myself agreeable, for perhaps the last time in my life."

"You have not exerted yourself much in that way as yet, this evening."

"No; I have felt too cowed and humiliated; but I cannot bear to see people sit silent and gloomy, so I shall try to forget myself now. I trust you can condescend to play at the small games I am going to introduce."

"I am at your service in this, as in all things," said Stephen, rising to let her pass.

Beatrice did not speak, but the curl of her lip was expressive. She walked up to the different groups, and, with more animation than she had hitherto shown, began to explain the game which was to be played. It was that called "Public Opinion," which is thus conducted : a person goes out of the room, taking upon himself the character of some animate or inanimate object, chosen by common consent; a second person, during his absence, collects the opinions of the party about him, under his assumed name ; and the point lies in the remarks being made to hit some real characteristic of the individual himself, whilst at the same time they apply to the part he enacts. The more severe and cutting the opinions are, the more amusing the game is considered.

Mr. Ashton, ever ready to make himself conspicuous, volunteered first to stand the brunt of "Public Opinion." He went out as a picture, and when he returned, Beatrice, who had collected the remarks about him, began, according to the rules of the game, to repeat them to him, leaving him to guess from whom they had proceeded. She told him, first, that some one had said " green was the predominant colour in his composition."

" Now, upon my word, this is too bad," said Mr. Ashton, looking round the room, laughing and colouring; " who can have said such a thing? I do believe it was yourself, Miss Clyde—you are always so severe—yes, I am sure it was you."

" No," returned Beatrice; " you have lost that guess; well, another person said you would improve with age."

" Ah! ah! that was Mr. Carleton."

" Wrong again. Another," proceeded Beatrice, " said you ought to be hung with your face to the wall."

" Miss Jessie Lyttelton, I am sure."

" No, indeed," said Beatrice; and she

went on declaring various opinions, which Mr. Ashton tried in vain to allot to their respective owners.

Most of them were the reverse of complimentary, which caused Mr. Menteith to remark to Mrs. Carleton, near whom he was sitting, "that he thought the game rather an unpleasant one."

"I think so too," she answered, "and I never introduce it. But Miss Clyde, and a few more who can give sharp answers, naturally like it. For my part, I think it gives great scope for rude and impertinent things to be said, and it makes those who are not very quick, or not confident enough to say what they think, feel very uncomfortable."

"I wonder any one is persuaded to go out," said Mr. Menteith, "to be a laughing-stock for the whole room. Just look how absurd that young man looks, trying to guess who said he was a caricature!"

"I don't care for him," said Mrs. Carleton. "He considers it flattering to have even rude things said of him, if they are said by young ladies."

"I suppose he thinks they say them to conceal their true opinions," said Mr. Menteith.

"A person said you were transparent," pursued Beatrice, when Mr. Ashton had made a wrong conjecture about the last-mentioned remark.

"Ha! now who could that be?" said Mr. Ashton. "A gentleman, 1 am positive. I should not wonder," said Mr. Ashton, his eyes wandering vaguely round the room, "if Mr. Menteith were the person."

He was right, though he had spoken at random, and chiefly because he had not guessed Mr. Menteith before.

"By the laws of the game, you will have to go out next time," said Mrs. Carleton.

" Shall I ? I shall try to make over my post to some one else."

" No, you will not be allowed," said Mrs. Carleton. And so it proved. For when Mr. Ashton had heard all the opinions about him, it was unanimously decreed that Mr. Menteith should next undergo the ordeal. He tried to get off, but yielded at last, though with visible unwillingness.

" What am I to be ?" he asked, as he was leaving the room. Various things were suggested and cast aside. At last some one mentioned a ship, and the idea was favourably received.

" One can say so much about a ship, you know," said Jessie Lyttelton, "about the rigging, and sails, and lots of things."

" I think very little can be said about a ship which will apply to me," said Mr. Menteith. " Surely you can think of something better ?"

"Oh! you don't know the resemblances we shall find out," said Mr. Carleton.

"Well, I am a novice at the game," said Mr. Menteith, "but if I may be allowed a choice in the matter I would rather not be a ship."

"All the more reason why you should be one," said Mr. Carleton. "I have already fixed upon my opinion, and I cannot afford to have any alteration."

"Nor I," said Jessie. "My opinion is quite ready."

"I suppose I *must* be a ship, then," said Mr. Menteith, "so I shall sail away till I am wanted," and, with a forced laugh, he left the room.

When he was gone there was a debate as to who should collect the opinions. Beatrice refused to undergo the labour a second time, in reality because she did not wish to repeat to Mr. Menteith what other people said about him—and Jessie Lyttelton at last was appointed to succeed her.

When it was Beatrice's turn to declare her opinion she had not one ready.

"Do, some one, help me," she said, looking round.

"The idea of helping Miss Clyde is quite absurd," said Mrs. Newton. "She is generally so quick with her answers that she can furnish them for other people. One is at a loss to understand how she can be puzzled."

"Then do, Mrs. Newton, help me now, and I will help you another time," said Beatrice.

"I, my dear! really I am so stupid; however, you might say that the ship had been in South America — on the South American coast, I mean."

"Ah! I see! of course I might say a ship had been anywhere; so I think I will say it has been amongst those islands Mr. Desmond talked about."

"The Fow-Chow Islands?" said Jessie.

"Yes—say," Beatrice paused an instant —"say the ship has visited the Fow-Chow Islands."

Jessie went on to some one else, and after a short time Mr. Menteith was summoned.

"Some one says," began Jessie, "that you are a ship that will always keep afloat, and steer clear of rocks and shoals."

"Indeed! I suppose I ought to consider that complimentary," said Stephen, smiling, so as to show his perfect set of teeth, but with a scowl gathering on his brow; "that opinion has come, I fancy, from Mr. Carleton."

"Wrong," said Jessie. "Another person says you know when you are in a good port."

"Ha, ha, very witty, I am sure!" said Stephen, laughing uncomfortably; "that was Mr. Ashton, I should think."

"No! you are still wrong; well, it is

said that it is evident you have been lately done up, fresh painted and new rigged."

"It must have required a very discriminating person to say that," said Mr. Menteith; "some one of very extended observation in life." He looked round, and there was a glance of anger in his eyes, though his voice was modulated to a tone of half-satirical pleasantry; "perhaps, Miss Jessie, the opinion is your own."

Jessie shook her head, and continued, "Another person says you are a ship to bear down all before you."

Mr. Menteith looked for a moment at Beatrice, and then it struck him that she was not likely to have expressed such an opinion, even if she had formed it; so he guessed Dora Lyttelton.

He was wrong, and Jessie went on—

"It is said that you are—had—oh dear! what was that punning one about a fright? I cannot remember it."

"I can imagine it, I dare say," said Mr. Menteith—"that I was a great fright, perhaps."

"Oh, I am sure no one could say anything so rude," said Mrs. Newton; "surely, my dear, you can recollect what it was."

"It was something of the kind," said Jessie; "but I have spoilt it in the telling —having a great freight, or something like that."

"As fair as most puns are," said Mr. Menteith, blandly; "and quite allowable under the circumstances. Who is guilty of punning? I think Mr. Ashton looks as if it were his."

"You are always guessing me," said Mr. Ashton, "and you are wrong again."

"Some one says you are laden with treasure from other climes," said Jessie.

"Ah! a lady, I think—Mrs. Carleton."

"No; another says you have visited the Fow-Chow Islands."

An attentive observer might have seen Mr. Menteith start slightly as this sentence was uttered, and an expression of extreme annoyance pass across his face. The lines about his mouth grew harsher, and his eyes, with cat-like vigilance, scrutinized each member of the party. For a single instant he fixed them upon Beatrice, and she felt at once that he knew she had made the remark, though why it should so much irritate him she could not guess. She had said it with scarcely any meaning, though influenced, perhaps half-consciously, by some vague idea, drawn from Mr. Desmond's speeches, that Stephen knew something of that voyage of his amongst the Fow-Chow Islands.

Mr. Menteith did not allow his emotion to be long perceptible; in fact, no one but a person interested in watching him would have been likely to observe the change of his countenance and manner.

He said, almost immediately—

"I fancy some young lady, impressed with Mr. Desmond's eloquence, must have imagined me in the Fow-Chow Islands. Was it Miss Constable?"

"No," answered Jessie. "It is said, also, that you are a merchant-vessel."

"The best remark that has been made— Mrs. Newton's, I fancy."

"Yes—you are right at last. Another person was afraid you did not belong to the Royal Navy."

Here was another speech which was evidently displeasing to Mr. Menteith. He changed colour, and his attitudes betrayed restlessness, and some embarrassment. He kept his smile, however, and said—

"Was that opinion Colonel Morley's?"

"No," returned Jessie; and she repeated several more opinions—some vague and meaningless, others decidedly uncomplimentary, though not likely to rouse any feeling save amusement in any but a remarkably touchy nature.

Mr. Menteith did not guess many, and when all had been said Jessie told him from whom they had proceeded.

"It was Colonel Morley who said you could keep afloat, and steer clear of rocks and shoals," said Jessie. " Mr. Heywood remarked that you knew when you were in a good port; and it was Mr. Carleton who said you were lately done up," &c.

" Ha!" said Stephen, glancing stealthily across the room at Mr. Carleton, who did not appear to notice him.

"The one about the freight," continued Jessie, " was said by my brother Fred. Mrs. Clyde's was the one about being laden with treasures from foreign climes ; and Miss Clyde said you had visited the Fow-Chow Islands."

Again Stephen gave Beatrice a searching

look ; but he directly resumed his attentive
manner of listening to Jessie.

"Mr. Ashton said he thought you did not
belong to the Royal Navy," she went on,
repeating in succession the whole of the
opinions, with the names of their owners.

The game was continued for some time
longer — several people going out. Mr.
Menteith never thoroughly entered into it,
and he and Mrs. Carleton sympathised with
each other in disapproval. Beatrice went
out as a lamp, and Stephen listened to all
that was said of her with jealous attention.
When some one said that she frequently
appeared under a shade, he looked eagerly
into the faces of those whom he suspected,
and was relieved when he found the observation had been made by Mrs. Newton,
whom he did not suppose capable of any
covert meaning. He was truly glad when
the guests had departed—he was not fond
of this kind of society, though he was a

man who enjoyed conversation in a small
circle. He could talk sensibly on almost
any topic; but he had not much of the
small change of society about him; and the
"chaff," which he found so great an ingre-
dient in the talk of the younger men he met,
was unbearable to him. He shrank from
joking, and from anything like personal
allusion; and it annoyed him greatly to
find Beatrice listening to such folly.

She, in truth, only cared for making the
evening pass quickly, and avoiding private
dialogues with her betrothed. When all
had retired, she went towards Mr. Menteith,
to say good night to him; but he followed
her from the room, and when they were in
the hall, said to her:

" What was the reason you made that
speech about the Fow-Chow Islands?"

He was so visibly in earnest that Beatrice
was surprised.

" What was my reason?—what was the

reason of most of the speeches?" she said
—" the want of something to say. I should
think I could scarcely have.chosen anything
more inoffensive."

" No—perhaps—of course." Stephen's
words came forth in a confused, incoherent
manner. "But—it was odd you should
imagine me in such a place! However, I
remember Mr. Desmond's lecture made an
impression upon you; but I fancied you
might have taken up some idea——"

"What idea could I take up?" said
Beatrice, raising her eyes, and looking
steadily at him. "I was not likely to think
you had really been in the Fow-Chow
Islands, though, for anything I know, you
may have been. I have never heard much
about your earlier life."

"You have not cared to hear," said
Stephen, recovering his equanimity a little.
"I wish you did. But some day, perhaps,
I shall tell you everything. It will not in-

clude, however, a description of the Fow-Chow Islands," he added, in a lighter tone, "I was puzzled to know what had made you think of them—that was all."

"It was difficult for me to say anything," said Beatrice. "I could not express my real thoughts—I have had no cause to form any opinion of you which you would like to hear, or I should choose to declare, before such a circle. Good night."

And shaking hands coldly, she proceeded up-stairs.

"When will this be altered?" said Stephen to himself, following her with his eyes—eyes full of a love which it mortified him to own, either to her or to himself, so small did her indifference make him feel. But he did love her, with all the ardour of which his nature—a strange compound of strength and weakness—was capable—an ardour, which even his very greatest weakness, his vanity, helped to foster. It would be a

triumph, he thought, to win her love—to
out-do in her estimation the gay and handsome men who had tried, he believed, to
gain her heart—to measure himself, with
his puny stature and irregular features,
against Lionel Constable, with his magnifi-
cent proportions and statuesque face. True,
Beatrice had avowed that she was bound to
him, but that did not satisfy him—he longed
for her love.   It was as he had told her—
she had fascinated him on the night of his
arrival ; and he had then resolved that she
should be his in reality, as well as in name.
The empty form they had gone through—
the prospect of its speedy renewal, could
not give him any rest or satisfaction, whilst
her cold demeanour endured.   He believed,
certainly, that she would do her duty as a
wife ; but it would be a mere barren duty
—the submission of a slave to her master—
not what he panted for from Beatrice.

No ; he longed to see her eyes lit up by

that fire which love kindled in his own far less expressive orbs. He thirsted to know that her heart beat with the wild, almost painful throbs that agitated his—to feel that her whole soul was filled with the same strange half torment, half bliss, which penetrated his at the sense of her very presence, the merest touch of her hand—oh ! to grasp that little hand, to feel it, even in the slightest degree, return the pressure of his—to hold her in his arms, unresisting—to press his lips on hers—to rouse at length an answering warmth in hers, and make them meet his kiss in involuntary rapture—close—close—in the first moment of awakened love !

END OF VOL. II.

R. BORN, PRINTER, GLOUCESTER STREET, REGENT'S PARK.

www.ingramcontent.com/pod-product-compliance
Lightning Source LLC
Chambersburg PA
CBHW031042120726
47905CB00007B/2278